HER WEREWOLF ENFORCER

WEREWOLF GUARDIAN ROMANCE SERIES

JODI VAUGHN

CHAPTER 1

"*A*re you ready for this, Brutus? The very first official meeting with our new Pack Master, Barrett Middleton." Killian Black shoved another chocolate-coated cookie in his mouth and sighed. He fell into step with his fellow Louisiana Assassin and savored the sugary goodness.

The dawn was just breaking over New Orleans, and the cooler weather had crept up in the South just a few days ago. It had gone from a balmy ninety degrees to a cool sixty-seven. "I hope Barrett doesn't make us clock in. I heard he made the Arkansas Guardians clock in." Killian loved his job as an Assassin. He only worked, alongside his two other Assassins, when someone needed executing for violating Pack Law.

He, Brutus, and Lorcan had a rhythm when it came to being Assassins. They worked in synchronicity like a finely tuned machine that always dealt out judgement and execution when they were ordered to. Which wasn't that often and not since Barrett Middleton had come into the office of Louisiana Pack Master.

"If we have to clock in, then you'll be out of a job. Your sorry ass is always late." Brutus continued down the street toward Barrett's house. He cut his eyes at Killian and frowned. "Where did you get those cookies? I didn't see any like that at the Compound."

"That's because I swiped them all when Jacey brought them in this morning." He shoved another one in his mouth.

"She brought those for all of us." Lorcan caught up to them and punched Killian in the arm, loosening his hold on the sugary delicacies.

Lorcan caught two in one hand while Brutus caught the other.

"Hey. Those are mine." Killian scowled.

"You need to learn to be less selfish. When the Pack Master's wife brings a gift like this, you have to share." Lorcan took a bite and sighed. "Damn. This is really good."

"I know. Why do you think I didn't want to share?" Killian glared.

"Because you're an asshole," Brutus offered.

"Am not." Killian rolled his arm where Lorcan had slugged him. How was it his fault that he was a sugar addict? Alcohol and drugs were never his thing, but put a donut in front of him, and he'd cut off his big toe for a bite.

"And I'm not always late either." Killian glared at the two alphas who were more like brothers than coworkers.

"The last few weeks you've been late every time we've pulled out to patrol the area."

"Patrol." He grimaced. "We are Assassins. When have we ever patrolled? It's not in my job description" He looked at both of them. "Now, when we are hunting down a target to kill, have I ever been late for that?"

"No. But you did miss when you were trying to shoot Braxton with a silver bullet," Brutus pointed out.

"Which happened to be a good thing by the way. He was innocent." He lifted his chin.

"Yeah, well, you just happened to get lucky. That's all." Lorcan stopped at a local art vendor in Jackson Square and studied the painting.

Killian inhaled deep. The scent of beignets washed over him. "I love the smell of New Orleans."

"The smell of vomit and urine?" Lorcan arched his brow.

"No, dumbass. The scent of chicory coffee and sugar-coated beignets." He glanced at his watch and wondered if he had time for a quick bite.

"No," Lorcan scowled.

"What?" He gave him his best innocent look.

"You're not getting a donut. Or anything else to eat for that matter. We are not going to be late for this meeting with Barrett." Lorcan groused.

"It's not like we haven't had meetings with him before. He's been Pack Master for almost three months." Killian didn't know what the big fucking deal was anyway. "Besides, we've not had any orders to assassinate anyone since he became Pack Master. I mean, I don't miss Boudier one bit, and I'm glad that fucker is dead, but to tell you the truth I'm getting kind of bored."

"That explains the spare tire you are starting to get." Brutus poked him hard in the stomach.

"Spare tire?" He stopped in his tracks and rubbed his stomach. He didn't feel any extra inches of fat. He did read somewhere that when people gain weight, they never notice until it was too late. He turned sideways and studied his reflection in the shop window.

"Come on, lazy ass," Lorcan called over his shoulder.

He caught the eye of a young female carrying an armful of flowers.

"Excuse me." He shot her a smile. She stopped. A blush spread across her cheeks.

"I need your honest opinion. Do you think I look a bit flabby?" He leaned down and whispered.

She shook her head. "I think you look perfect." She hurried away, giggling as she went.

He lifted his chin and stared at the other Assassins. He smirked. "Yep, just what I thought. Still perfection."

CHAPTER 2

Barrett Middleton pushed the coffee cup away and grabbed Jacey around her waist as she walked past the dining room table. He pulled her into his lap.

"What are you doing?" She giggled and leaned into his embrace. "You have a meeting in ten minutes."

"I can think of a better use of my time. Like satisfying you." He nuzzled her ear. God, he loved the way she smelled. He was constantly in a state of arousal whenever she was near. And when she wasn't, she was always on his mind. Her pregnancy had made her even more irresistible.

"I want more than ten minutes of your attention." She turned in his arms. Wrapping her arms around his neck, she pulled him in for a long kiss.

Her sweet taste exploded on his tongue. She sighed as she held him close.

He loved the little sounds she made whenever he kissed her.

The doorbell sent a melodious chime throughout the house.

"Fuck." He pulled away and scowled.

She laughed. "I would get yourself under control before you meet with the Assassins. You don't want the pretty one to think this is for him." She gently squeezed his crotch.

"Which one do you think is pretty?"

He scowled. He pretty much already knew she was talking about Killian with his long, black hair, gray eyes, and rock star attire.

She laughed and shook her head.

"Do you think Killian is pretty?" He growled.

"I love it when you get jealous like this." She picked up his coffee cup and deposited it in the kitchen sink. He watched her tight ass as she left the room.

He looked up at the ceiling. He took some deep breaths and thought about accounting. Once he'd gotten his arousal under control, he walked over and opened the massive glass and wrought iron door.

The three Assassins stood on the other side.

"You're early." Barrett scowled.

"See. We're not late at all." Killian lifted his chin at Brutus and Lorcan.

Lorcan glanced at his watch. "We are two minutes early." He met Barrett's gaze. "Hope that's okay."

"Come in." He moved away and let them enter. His gaze lingered a little longer on Killian.

"Come into the living room, and I'll have Jacey bring some coffee."

"Does she have any of those cookies left?" Killian asked hopefully, his eyes shining with excitement.

Irritated, he glared.

"No." Barrett growled softly. He didn't want Killian anywhere near Jacey's cookies. Or anything else of hers. "Killian, you let your hair grow out."

"Felt like I needed a change. You know how it is." Killian smiled.

6

Barrett narrowed his eyes on the Were.

"You have to forgive our friend, Barrett." Lorcan shook his head. "Killian is a sugar addict."

"Is that right?" Barrett glared.

"I am not." Killian gave Lorcan a hard look. "I just appreciate cookies…"

"And cakes, and candy bars, and soda, and donuts…" Brutus deadpanned.

Killian grimaced. "I'm sure our Pack Master isn't interested in my eating habits."

The Assassins waited until Barrett sat. Then they all took a seat. Barrett leaned back in his chair. An idea blossomed in his mind. He rubbed his chin, aware that all eyes were on him. "Actually, Killian's sugar addiction might come in handy."

The room grew silent. He let the silence stretch. He had been Pack Master long enough to know the power of the unspoken word.

"I need someone to investigate something." Barrett finally spoke.

"Investigate? Shouldn't you be asking the Guardians? Not the Assassins?" Killian asked.

Lorcan and Brutus turned and glared at Killian.

"What?" Killian looked around. "Don't give me that look, Lorcan. You know that you and Brutus were wondering the same thing." He relaxed in his chair. "No offense, Barrett."

"Rather be out assassinating Weres, would you, Killian?" Barrett cocked his head.

"That's why we are called Assassins and not babysitters." Killian chuckled.

Brutus stood, walked up behind Killian, and slapped the back of his head.

"Owwww. What's that for?" Killian rubbed his head.

"For being disrespectful." Brutus snarled.

"I'm not being disrespectful. Barrett asked my opinion. I thought when we got rid of Boudier, Barrett wanted to have an open dialogue with his Assassins." Killian scowled.

"And since Barrett has been Pack Master of Louisiana, we've not been sent on any missions to assassinate anyone," Lorcan said between gritted teeth.

Barrett caught the look of confusion on Killian's face. "Killian, are you happy with your job as Assassin?"

Killian's smile began to fade. Barrett could see the little hamster turning in his head.

"Don't answer that." Barrett held up his hand. "I was going to send all three of you to investigate a situation for me. But I think now that Killian has voiced his complaints . . . I've changed my mind."

CHAPTER 3

*S*hit. He'd said something wrong. Not that it was the first time, but damn, never to a Pack Master.

"I wasn't complaining." Killian stood and swallowed. "I love my job. I have no complaints at all." He looked at the other two Assassins for help.

Brutus gave him a look of disgust. The Were probably thought Killian was acting like a little bitch. And Lorcan. God help him, Lorcan looked like he was ready to skin him alive. Which was saying something considering that Lorcan's brother Lucien was nearly killed that way.

"I had considered sending all three of you to do some recon near Natchez."

"Natchez? That's in Mississippi. Wouldn't that be Jack Welbourn's problem since he's the Pack Master of Mississippi?" Brutus asked.

"It would. Except he's still a little miffed at me for not capturing and returning the Witch of Yazoo City." Barrett rubbed his temple.

"The Witch helped bring you back from the dead. I

thought he would be appreciative." Lorcan leaned back into his seat.

"He would except that she keeps leaving a trail of bodies in her wake. If we can do some recon on a suspected Were drug operation in Natchez, it would smooth things over with Welbourn."

"We'd be glad to go. No problem." Killian offered.

"Good. Cause I'm just sending you, Killian. I have different jobs for Brutus and Lorcan." Barrett trained his gaze on him.

"Wait. They're not going with me?" Killian looked at Brutus and Lorcan. "We've always gone on missions together."

"This isn't an assassination mission, Killian." Barrett glared. "Are you refusing an order?"

His gut clenched. His stupid mouth had almost gotten him in trouble.

"No. Of course not. I'll do the job." Killian lifted his chin. "What kind of place is this? A red wolf hideout? A meth lab? A sex trafficking operation?"

Barrett grinned and handed him a pamphlet. On the front was a picture of a chocolate cake. "It's a bakery."

CHAPTER 4

illian stuffed a pair of jeans into the leather saddle bag of his Harley Davidson Breakout and growled.

A fucking bakery. He was on a mission to bust Little Debbie.

He fastened the straps on the bag and clenched his jaw. He should have known his smart-ass mouth was going to get him in trouble one day.

He just didn't expect it to be with the new Pack Master of Louisiana.

Brutus leaned a hip on his own black Breakout. "Bring me back a Twinkie Cake."

Killian jerked his gaze up to him. "There's no such thing as a Twinkie Cake, dumbass."

"Yes, there is." Brutus straightened. "I saw it on Pinterest."

Lorcan chuckled as he walked up to join them. "While you're at it, I'll take a dozen strawberries and cream cupcakes. I fucking love strawberry."

Killian stood and curled his hands into fists. "How about I shove my…"

"Enough," Brutus held up his hands. "Shit man. For someone with a smart-ass mouth, you sure can't take a joke."

Killian forced his hands to unclench. He took a deep breath and looked around. "Do you know how this is going to ruin my reputation if it gets around?"

"What reputation?" Lorcan snorted.

"Dude. I'm an Assassin. If this gets around that I'm investigating a fucking bakery, I'll never get laid again." Killian lowered his voice. "This will ruin my street cred. Forever."

"You need a life, Killian." Lorcan's bored tone indicated he didn't realize how serious the situation was.

Killian turned his glare on Lorcan. "If Barrett had told you to leave behind all your Assassin talents, and go investigate a place that makes cupcakes and cookies, are you seriously telling me that you wouldn't have an issue with it?"

"I'm saying that after years of executing criminal Weres, some more deserving than others, I would jump at the chance at a reprieve of doing something mindless. Like checking out a bakery and still getting paid." Lorcan sighed. "It would give my conscious a vacation from all the blood I've spilled." Lorcan shrugged. "Not judging. But some of us are more cold-blooded than others. That's just how we're made."

Killian studied Lorcan's face. It was the first time he saw regret in his friend's eyes.

"Don't sweat it, Killian." Lorcan clapped him on the arm. "Just think about this assignment as a vacation from our normal duties. You'll be back to assassinating the bad guys in no time."

Killian watched Lorcan's retreating back. Lorcan did make a point.

"Don't forget, Killian. Twinkie Cake." Brutus barked out his command before pushing off the Harley.

CHAPTER 5

Killian was awake before the sun came up over the sleepy town of Natchez, Mississippi. He had ridden into Natchez on fumes last night. He had gassed up at the small gas station before hunting down a hotel room. It was springtime and a lot of the hotels had booked up due the Spring Pilgrimage Tour. The annual spring event brought people from all over the world to tour all the plantation homes in the city.

After several attempts, he finally managed to snag a room at the Monmouth Plantation. He would rather been in a hotel where he could come and go without bringing too much attention to himself, but they were all sold out.

A bed and breakfast would have to do.

He locked his room and headed downstairs to the dining area for breakfast. He hoped they would have something sweet to go with his morning coffee.

"Good morning, Mr. Black. I hope you slept well." The owner, Mrs. Spell, flashed him a smile and blushed as she patted her gray hair into place.

"Hello, Mrs. Spell. I slept like a rock." He grinned. He

spied the coffee pot and changed his direction. "Ah, just what I need." He lifted the carafe and poured the dark brew into a white coffee cup.

"We order that straight from France. It's a special roast." Mrs. Spell uncovered the foil from a casserole dish. "For breakfast there is a sausage and egg casserole." She pointed to a bowl of fresh cut watermelon, strawberries, and blueberries. "Fresh fruit from our local farmers. And…" She lifted the lid off a cake platter. "Homemade cinnamon rolls that will literally melt in your mouth."

He sighed. And fell in love with the old woman. "Did you make those?"

"Oh no. I have a young lady, Lilliana, who made them." She handed him a white plate with tiny blue flowers around the rim. "She went to culinary school. She's been such a great help here at Monmouth Plantation."

"I'm sure." He scooped up some of the casserole, ignored the fruit, and snagged three large cinnamon rolls. He took his feast to the large antique table in the dining room. Thankfully, all the other guests were not up yet so he had the whole room to himself.

"Killian, are you here on business?" She eased herself into a chair across from him.

His shoulders slumped a little. He paused the sweet roll inches from his mouth and forced polite conversation out of his mouth. "I'm here to unwind."

"I figured that. I have excellent instinct. I could tell when you walked in last night that you are someone important."

He froze and held the woman's gaze.

She leaned in and whispered. "I know who you are."

"You do?" She was human. Not even a werewolf. Hell, most civilian Weres never knew what the famed Louisiana Assassins even looked like. How the hell did she know who he was?

"You're one of those famous rock stars." She smiled and lifted her chin in victory.

He relaxed and smiled. "How'd you know?" He took a large bite of the sweet roll. The sugar exploded on his tongue like a thousand fireworks on the Fourth of July.

"I could tell by the long hair and all that black you are wearing." She shrugged. "But don't worry. I will keep your secret. I won't tell any of the other guests. I know how important it is for someone like you to have time to unwind from your work." She got up and patted his shoulder. "Enjoy your time here at Monmouth."

"Thanks. I will." He finished off the sweet roll and watched Mrs. Spell's departing back.

He lingered over coffee. His gaze landed on a small display stand outside of the dining room. He stood and walked over to the display.

He scanned the different colored pamphlets and pulled out one that said Natchez Bakery. He pulled out the paper and found the address.

The same address as the bakery that Barrett wanted him to check out.

He stuck the paper in the pocket of his black leather jacket.

This job looked like it was going to be easy peasy.

CHAPTER 6

$\mathcal{L}$illiana Beckway propped open the back door of the Natchez Bakery with a brick and opened the trunk of her beat-up Nissan. She carefully picked up one of the four white cake boxes and slowly walked inside the kitchen.

"What do you have for me today, Lilliana? I hope one of those is a Hummingbird Cake." Emmett Reece, the owner of the bakery, looked down from his six-foot-four-inch height and narrowed his gaze.

Even though he was skinny as a rail, the man still intimidated her. After spending so much time in French pastry school, she had thought she would be further along in her career and making her dreams come true. She hadn't realized it would be hard to find a job in Natchez when people didn't want the exotic; they wanted the comfort of old standbys. Like her Hummingbird Cakes.

"I have two Hummingbird Cakes and two cream cheese pound cakes with orange blossom icing." She smiled and put the cake down.

"Orange icing? What about regular cream cheese icing?

That's what Southerners want. Not all that fancy-schmancy stuff." He glared and opened the top of the cake box. His glare left and instead a look of appreciation spread across his face.

Emmett Reece might want to find fault with everything she did, but it was his customers clamoring for her cakes that made him order from her every week.

While she loved the free rein she had at Monmouth, she did appreciate the extra money she got at the Natchez Bakery.

What she didn't like was the fact that Emmett never gave her credit for her own cakes. Emmett bought her cakes but marketed them as an original creation of Natchez Bakery.

She finished unloading the desserts and lingered in the kitchen. She shoved an escaped strand of hair behind her ear and cleared her throat. "You know, I would really appreciate an acknowledgement when you set out the cakes for display. A simple place card that says an original by Lilliana Beckway would be nice. You know, just to let people know who the creator is."

Emmett quietly placed the cakes on decorative glass cake stands and garnished them with a string of plastic honey-suckles.

Lilliana cringed. She hated when he messed up her beautiful desserts with plastic crap. She wished he would just leave well enough alone.

He turned and looked down his long crooked nose at her. "How would it look for Natchez Bakery to sell something that wasn't made right here?" He cocked his head.

"I understand but I am trying to make a name for myself, and baking all these desserts without an acknowledgment is not the direction I want to go." She lifted her chin. She needed to stand her ground.

"I see." He turned and walked into his office.

Her stomach dropped. Dear God, he was going to not order any more desserts, and she was not going to have the extra money. She needed that extra money to send to her mother in Louisiana. Her mother had raised her after Lilliana's father left when she was young. Her single mother wanted her daughter to have opportunities that she had not had.

Her mother had spent every dime, including her retirement, sending Lilliana to school.

It was now Lilliana's mission to pay every cent back to her mother so she could finally retire and live out the rest of her days in her small country house in Louisiana and take care of her goats and quilt instead of working as a nurse at the hospital. Her arthritis was getting worse as the years went by, but her sweet mama never complained.

Lilliana made it her mission to save any extra money she could.

For the last two years, she'd lived on next to nothing and took any extra work she could. It helped that she lived at Monmouth in a small cabin near the back of the house for free. When she went to Natchez Bakery to offer her cakes, Emmett had scoffed at first, but then once customers started requesting her desserts, he'd started ordering cakes from her every week.

Now with Emmett letting her go, she was going to have to find another source of extra income.

Maybe she could sell them herself. She sighed. It would take years to build up a client base and a lot of money to start her own bakery.

Money she didn't have.

Emmett came out of the office with an envelope in his hand. It was fatter than normal, and she already knew what that meant. It was her termination papers.

"You should be grateful for the opportunity you've had

here at Natchez Bakery." He held out the envelope to her. "People who are grateful get more. Even if it isn't in acknowledgments." He turned and headed to his office and shut the door.

She stood frozen with a pit in her stomach.

She glanced down at the envelope in her hands. She slowly opened it. And stared. Instead of termination papers, it was money. A lot of it.

She thumbed through the hundred-dollar bills and counted. One thousand dollars.

The office door flew open, and Emmett stuck his head out the door. "Friday, I want six Hummingbird Cakes. It's springtime and customers want things that make them think of Easter. Hummingbird Cake is one of those things." He slammed the door.

She looked down at the envelope filled with cash.

She wasn't fired. She was getting a raise. All she had to do was shove down her pride and accept the fact she wasn't going to get any credit for baking for the Natchez Bakery.

She thought of her mama and all she'd sacrificed for Lilliana.

Now it was her chance to sacrifice. If that meant no credit for baking most of the cakes in Natchez Bakery, then so be it.

CHAPTER 7

*K*illian parked his Harley Davidson Breakout along the street in a parking spot and threw the kickstand. He eased off his bike and stood in front of the Natchez Bakery.

He observed a steady stream of customers going in and out of the store. Families, older women, and young couples would enter empty-handed and leave either with their arms full of cake boxes or hands full of cupcakes.

His gaze followed a young woman carrying a perfect strawberry cupcake in her hand. Her tongue snaked out and swiped across the icing. She caught him looking and gave him a sultry smile.

He returned the smile and wondered if he could talk her out of her cupcake.

She kept walking but threw a suggestive gaze across her shoulder.

He hated to tell her, but right now he was more interested in the cupcake in her hand than *her* cupcake in her pants.

He looked back at the bakery. His mouth watered. Maybe

Barrett was right. Maybe this was right up his alley. Just an easy assignment with all the desserts he could eat.

He opened the door.

The scent of sugar and icing washed over him like a tempting caress.

He trained his gaze on the glass display counter. It was twenty feet long and any kind of dessert was there for the taking, for the right price of course.

He waited for a family of five to move so he could start his perusal. He wanted to go from end to end before he decided what he wanted to eat. Besides, it would give him time to do some recon. Dessert and recon, that's totally what he was doing.

"Can I help you sir?" A tall, lanky human standing on the other side of the counter asked in a low voice. It was the tone of someone trying to tell him to hurry up and put your order in and move along. Killian wasn't ready to move along. Mr. Lanky was going to have to wait.

"I'm looking. I want to look at all my options before making my choice." Killian cocked his head. "That okay with you?"

"Yes, of course, sir. Take all the time you need." The lanky man stepped away from the counter and walked down to help a young couple ordering some cupcakes.

Killian's eyes roamed the display case. There were flavors of every cookie imaginable. Cupcakes were decorated with perfect icing with exotic names like Strawberry Cream Cheese Delight and Chocolate Turtle Explosion. His mouth watered as he moved down the line, taking his time.

After the cupcakes were cakes. Large, beautiful, diabetic-inducing cakes. His eyes landed on one beautifully decorated with a weird-looking plastic honeysuckle around the bottom. He frowned. His gaze drifted down to the name. Hummingbird Cake.

What the fuck was a Hummingbird Cake?

He pressed his finger to the glass. Without looking up, he spoke. "I'll take that one."

Mr. Lanky hurried down the counter and looked from the cake to Killian. "Would you like a piece, sir?"

Killian looked Mr. Lanky in the eye. "No. The whole thing."

It took about a minute to pay for the cake in cash.

He knew he hadn't thought things through when he walked out of the store and back to his motorcycle.

It took another ten minutes to figure out how to get a whole cake back to the Monmouth Plantation on a Harley Davidson. He grabbed some bungie cord out of his luggage bag and secured the cake to the back of his bike. He glanced up at the sun. Although it was now a cool seventy degrees, it was bright, and he knew the sun would quickly melt the cream cheese frosting if it stayed outside too long.

He straddled his bike. He really hadn't seen anything unusual at the bakery. He figured he could take the cake back to his room at Monmouth and eat a piece or three before he headed back out to do some more recon. While he was enjoying his cake, he'd give Barrett a quick update. Hell, maybe Mrs. Spell had some of that great coffee set out. He couldn't think of anything better than cake and coffee.

He smiled, started the bike, and headed back to the bed and breakfast.

CHAPTER 8

*K*illian parked his bike and grabbed his cake. His mouth was watering at the tempting scent of the sugar. He didn't think he would wait until he was inside. He spotted the small garden just a few feet away. The perfect place for a snack. He changed direction and found a quiet path that led to a concrete seat beside a small pond. He sat down and opened the top of the box.

"You must have bought that cake at Natchez Bakery," a feminine voice said softly.

He frowned and turned at the intrusion. All he wanted was to eat some cake in peace and quiet, not chat with a nosey stranger.

His gaze landed on a pair of the greenest eyes he'd ever seen. The female was tall and slender, with long hair the color of a midnight sky. She wore jeans that hugged her soft curves and showed off her long legs. She had on a black T-shirt with the word Angel spread across the chest. She eyed him as she stepped closer.

He closed his eyes and inhaled. Her scent hit him like a punch. She was human.

"I did. Do you want a piece?" He didn't take his eyes off her, which was unusual. He loved the ladies. He had been with women in every state, both Were and human. But when it came to his desserts, he never shared.

He frowned. Why the hell had he offered to share his cake with a female human?

Sweat popped out on his skin, and he pressed his hand to his head. Maybe he had the flu? Werewolves didn't get the flu, he reminded himself. Maybe he had some kind of rare wolf disease?

"Are you okay? You look kind of sick." She crossed her arms and studied him.

"Yeah. I'm alright." He glanced back down at his cake. "Have you ever eaten a cake from the Natchez Bakery?"

"Yes." She shrugged and glanced away. The spring wind caught her hair and lifted it into the air. Her scent curled in his nostrils.

He groaned. "You smell like sugar."

She lifted her hair to her nose and sniffed. "Really? I took a shower."

He shook his head and tried to clear his mind. "Maybe it's your shampoo," he mumbled and looked away.

"Are you going to eat your cake or what?" She seemed a little impatient and not at all into him.

Did she not have any kind of reaction to him? Hell, he could walk down the street and women would follow him, but Little Miss here looked like she had better places to be.

"I am." He waved for her to sit.

She shook her head. "I can't stay long. I have to get back to work. I have several guests that signed up for dinner."

"Wait, are you the cook here?" He watched her nod her head slowly.

"I am."

"So, you made those wonderful sweet rolls this morning." A smile stretched across his face.

"I did. Glad you enjoyed them. Mrs. Spells wants me to make more casseroles and less sweets…"

"No!" he said a little too quickly.

Her eyes widened.

"Sorry, it's just that those sweet rolls were the best thing I have ever put into my mouth." Suddenly he was flooded with images of putting her into his mouth. His body clenched with desire, and he fought the urge to shove her up against the tall shrubbery and kiss her until she was clawing at him.

"That's good to know." A grin settled on her beautiful lips. "So what are you waiting for?"

Shit. Did she have the ability to read his mind? Was she more than human? He didn't smell any other paranormal scent on her.

"Well? Are you going to eat that cake or what?" She crossed her arms impatiently.

"Yeah. Right. Of course." He grimaced. He'd certainly called that wrong.

He tried to focus on the sweetness in front of him. Oddly enough, he couldn't stop thinking about the female beside him.

"I'm Killian." He held out his hand.

"Just Killian?" She arched a brow.

"Killian Black." He was feeling a bit like a loser just holding his hand in the air.

"Lilliana Beckway." She took his hand.

Warmth shot from his hand straight to his chest and spread to his dick. He watched her eyes widen as she felt the sensation too.

She snatched her hand away. "The cake." She nodded. "I'm curious to hear your opinion."

Why had his body reacted that way? To a mere human?

"Right." He turned his attention back to the job at hand. "I don't have anything to cut it with." That wasn't true. There was a knife inside his boot, but the last time he used it was on a mission. It probably still had blood on it. Cake and blood didn't pair well together.

"Here." She pulled out a serrated knife from the back pocket of her jeans.

"Do you always carry weapons?" He narrowed his eyes.

"Just when I am getting ready to cook." She shrugged. "I'm making dinner tonight, and I need it to chop some vegetables for the side dish.

He nodded and took the knife.

He carefully cut into the cake, letting the knife slice into the layers.

He pulled out a thin slice of the cake. He could smell cinnamon, sugar, and bananas. "I wasn't expecting fruit," he said.

"You've never had Hummingbird Cake?"

"No."

She grinned. "Did you think there would be hummingbirds in there?"

"To be honest, I wasn't sure. It looked so good, I wouldn't care if it had crows baked in there."

She let out a laugh, breaking the tension in the small garden.

He lifted the cake to his mouth. Flavor exploded on his tongue on his at the first bite.

"Well?"

He chewed thoughtfully. Suddenly he bit down on something hard. Sweetness dissolved into bitterness. He grimaced and hurried to the nearest shrub. Poking his head through, he spit out the rest of the cake.

He wiped his mouth with the back of his hand and stood.

When he turned around, Lilliana was glaring at him. "So you didn't like it."

He shook his head. "Whatever was in that cake is not fit for consumption."

"What do you know? You're no expert." She curled her hands into fists and turned on her heel. She stormed back to the main house, cursing under her breath, but loud enough for him to hear.

"Perfect. Now she hates me." Killian grabbed the cake box and headed to the trash can by one of the cabins. He opened the lid and shoved the rest of the cake inside.

CHAPTER 9

*B*arrett drummed his fingers on his desk as he waited for Killian to answer his call. Just when he was about to hang up, the Were answered.

"Hello?"

"What took you so long? You have your head shoved in a box of donuts?" Barrett thundered.

"Actually, a cake box," Killian said sullenly.

"What?" Barrett glared. "Never mind. Did you find out anything about the Natchez Bakery?"

"I found out their cakes suck," Killian replied.

"What else? Did you see anything else going on? Did you check out their kitchen? Any hint of drug trafficking?" He rubbed his temple. A slow throb began building inside his brain.

"I walked in the front door. Looked around. And bought a cake. Which I severely regret."

"You did no recon." Barrett was trying very hard to keep his anger in check.

"Can't you just let one of the Guardians do some recon?

And when you find the culprit, I'll just assassinate them. It's kind of my jam."

"Killian," Barrett growled. "I understand that Louisiana Assassins under Boudier were paid killers…"

"Yes." The joy in Killian's voice was evident.

"But I'm not Boudier. I like to have all my information before I willy-nilly start killing everyone." Barrett closed his eyes and counted to ten.

"I know. I like you much better than Boudier. Trust me. It's just that I've been assassinating so long that I don't know anything else."

That was the problem. Barrett wanted the Assassins to see a different side of life out from under Boudier's control.

"Go back to the Natchez Bakery and get me some real recon."

"Yes, sir," Killian answered.

"And Killian? Don't buy any more cakes." Barrett ended the call.

*L*illiana wiped her hands on her jeans after she finished putting the finishing touches on the soup. Tonight, they had started out with six guests for dinner. At the last minute, another guest signed up, taking the total number, as well as her stress level, up.

"Go ahead and serve this while I start on the main course." She looked at Mrs. Spell. "I hope the guests understand the main course will take another twenty minutes to finish and plate. People these days don't know how to slow down and enjoy their meal."

"Don't worry, honey. I'll make sure to keep them talking. Especially that good-looking one."

"What good-looking one?" She jerked her gaze up to the older lady.

"The one that looks like a rock star." She waggled her gray eyebrows.

"Killian." Her stomach sank. She knew immediately who Mrs. Spell was talking about.

"Yes." Her smile widened. "I see you've met him. He's certainly a cutie, don't you think?"

"I think he's rude, with no taste in culinary arts. He probably eats gas station pastries and thinks it's the best he's ever had." She glared at the filets she'd just thrown on the grill. Thankfully all her guests had order either rare or medium rare so at least the steaks wouldn't take very long to cook. She'd already prepped the twice baked potatoes and wilted spinach with parmesan so those wouldn't take long at all.

"He's a man, honey. They all think gas station food is wonderful." Mrs. Spell grabbed a couple of soup bowls. "Besides, once he has had your dessert tonight, you'll make a changed man out of him." Mrs. Spell headed out into the dining room.

"If he hated my Hummingbird Cake at the bakery, he'll hate the crème brûlée I'm serving tonight," she mumbled to herself.

She turned her attention on the food and set her timer.

Mrs. Spell walked back into the kitchen carrying the empty soup bowls on a platter. "Your French Onion Soup was a hit. No one left a drop in their bowl and even the lady who said she hated onion loved it."

"That's good." She felt the tension slide off her shoulders. She finished plating the main course and topped it with a garnish. She stepped back and admired her work.

"Oh, Lilliana. That looks amazing. And smells divine." Mrs. Spell clapped her on the back. "Hiring you was the best decision I ever made. Business has picked up with you working here."

"I'm glad." She gave the older woman a smile. Mrs. Spell had given her a job when no one else would. The pay wasn't great, but she was also getting a free place to stay. Plus, Mrs. Spell didn't mind her cooking for the Natchez Bakery on the side.

She turned her attention to making crème brûlée. Dessert was her favorite part of being a chef. Something about turning ingredients into something sweet and comforting felt like her calling in this world.

Some people could heal with medicine. She preferred to heal the world with dessert.

When Mrs. Spell carried the dessert out to the guests, Lilliana grabbed a wine glass out of the cabinet. She pulled out a bottle of Malbec that she'd bought earlier that day. Unscrewing the top, she poured herself a liberal amount into the crystal.

She took a drink of the garnet-colored liquid. She closed her eyes as the liquid slid down her throat in a warm rush of flavor.

Laughter from the dining room drifted into the kitchen. She'd done good tonight. The guests were happy.

Which meant she should be happy.

She grabbed her glass and the bottle of wine. She opened the back door and slipped out into the backyard.

The bright spring day had dissolved into an inky-black night. The sweet scent of honeysuckle played on the cool night air.

She stepped into the garden. She walked down the stone pathway and stopped in the middle of the courtyard. She sat on the stone bench and placed the bottle beside her. She sipped on her wine and watched the water bubbling in the fountain.

"Want some company?" The deep male voice broke the silence of the night. Killian stepped off the path and in front of her.

Her heart sped up.

"Not really." She wanted to ignore the handsome man in front of her, but it was impossible. She reminded herself she was angry at him for how he'd reacted to eating her cake.

He eased his large frame beside her.

He stretched out his long legs clad in black jeans and

biker boots and looked at her with gray eyes. He was wearing a black leather jacket over a black shirt. Even his long hair was black.

"Mrs. Spell said you were responsible for making our dinner tonight. I wanted to find you and tell you it was the best meal I have ever had."

"Even the dessert?" She held his gaze and gritted her teeth.

"Especially the dessert." He grinned. "I'm an expert on desserts."

Her heart sped up faster and her breathing grew faster. She tried to tell herself her body was reacting to him because she was pissed and not because she was attracted to the handsome asshole.

"Really?" She tried to hold on to her anger about his spitting out her Hummingbird Cake, but he was so close and whatever cologne he was wearing was wreaking havoc on her lady parts.

"It's a fact." He picked up the wine bottle and gave her a wicked grin. "Mind sharing?"

She looked away and closed her eyes tight. The more he smiled, the more she wanted to do things she hadn't entertained in a while.

"Go ahead. But I didn't bring an extra glass."

"I thought ahead." He pulled a wine glass out of his jacket pocket. "I swung by the kitchen when I saw you leaving out the back door."

"You were watching me?" She swallowed. It had been a while since she had been so attracted to a guy. And she was never attracted to jerks like him.

She should date more, get kissed more often. That would certainly take the edge off her raging libido.

He held her gaze. Her stomach warmed.

"Of course I was watching you. Beautiful woman like

yourself. I bet you have a lot of admirers." He narrowed his eyes, as if he didn't like that idea. Not in the least.

Something about Killian threw her off her game. She'd always been street smart. She had casually dated when she had the time but never really had a serious relationship.

That's how she liked it. She had goals and dreams and didn't need a man to complete her.

Especially a hot guy like Killian. She'd learned her lesson from her mother.

Get an education. Follow your dreams. Be independent. But most importantly.

Never, ever rely on a man.

But she'd never been so instantly attracted to a guy before like she was to Killian. She cleared her throat and stood. "I appreciate your compliment on dinner. I hope you enjoy the rest of your evening." She tried to walk around him, but he caught her elbow.

Her breath caught in her throat.

"I was hoping to…" His voice trailed off. His pupils dilated. And another current of electricity shot through her from his point of contact.

Desire pulsed through her veins. Her breathing increased.

He let go of her elbow, then reached out and tucked a strand of hair behind her ear. His hand lingered. His fingertips cupped her cheek. "You smell delicious."

Her stomach warmed, and lust pooled between her legs. She inhaled deep. His scent beckoned to her, and she couldn't help but lean into his space.

Her anger and pride now forgotten was replaced with overwhelming lust.

His free hand rested on her hip and nudged her dangerously closer into his sinful body.

Her hands had a mind of their own and trailed up his

arms. She traced the sharp edge of every muscle under her fingertips.

He growled low and bent his head toward hers.

"What are we doing?" she whispered.

"We are doing what feels right." He bent his head and covered her mouth in a blistering kiss.

She opened her mouth, welcoming his hot tongue. It had been too long since she'd been kissed, and never like this.

Her fingers slid up past his shoulders, and she tangled them into his long hair. She moaned as his tongue slid against hers, kissing her hard and deep and without consequence.

Wicked images of them both naked and writhing against each other until they were wet with satisfied desire streaked through her head.

He moved his mouth to her neck.

"More. I need more." She pulled his mouth back to hers, and he ground his erection against her wet core.

He slid both hands to her ass and picked her up. She wrapped her legs around his lean waist and panted as he continued to kiss her.

He broke the kiss and stared into her eyes. He panted and his gray eyes were nearly black with desire. "You are so fucking beautiful."

Her heart shuddered, and she pulled his mouth back to hers. She tightened her heels around his waist and slid against his erection. Pleasure tingled through her clit.

"I know what you need." He pressed her back against the brick garden wall. He slid his jean-clad erection against her.

"Yes," she whispered as her head lolled back against the wall. Pleasure built with each glide against her clit.

"That feel good, baby?" He sucked the sensitive place against her neck. "I want to make you feel good."

"Yes." She dug her nails into his shoulders. "Please. More."

He growled and buried his face into her throat.

Pleasure built until a wave of desire spread through her wet heat and throughout every cell of her body. He continued to rock against her until she shivered in the after-shock of the orgasm

"Fuck." He nibbled at her neck and rocked against her. He moved fast against her as he found his own pleasure.

Breathing heavy, he buried his face into her neck. His hot breath licked across the shell of her ear.

He placed gentle kisses along her neck and cheek. When he let her feet touch the ground, she held onto his arms until she was strong enough to stand.

*K*illian tried to get his breathing under control. They hadn't even had sex but had managed to get each other off.

Strangely erotic. They were total strangers to each other yet he felt like he knew her all his life.

"That was...unexpected," she admitted.

"Really? I knew from the moment I met you that I wanted you." He stared into her soul. He couldn't lie. Not to her.

"I usually don't get off with males who hate my baking. It's this rule I have." She shook her head.

"Hate your baking? I told you I love your cooking." He frowned. What was she talking about?

"Tonight you did, but you spit..." She straightened at the sound of voices growing closer. She took a step back and patted her hair into place. "I have to go. I have some baking I have to do tonight for deliveries in the morning." She stepped away before he could grab her.

"Killian, there you are." Mr. Bruce Davis smiled and pushed his wide-rimmed glasses up on his nose. His wife,

Mattie, had her arm looped in his and was sipping on a glass of sherry.

"You ran off before you could have a cocktail." Mattie held her glass in the air. "I've never had such a wonderful meal or better companions to share it with."

"Yes, yes, Mattie. I quite agree. They certainly don't cook a meal like this in Philadelphia." Bruce patted his wife's hand.

"It was probably the best meal I have ever had as well." Killian ran his fingers through his hair and stared in the direction that Lilliana had taken off. He couldn't seem to figure her out. The sexual chemistry between them had been off the charts but afterward, he got the feeling she didn't like him very much.

It was a problem he wasn't used to having when it came to women.

"Mrs. Spell says the young lady who cooks for her went to culinary school and French pastry school," Mattie offered.

"It was money well spent in my humble opinion." Bruce nodded.

"Yes. Very well spent." Killian graced the couple with a smile. "If you will excuse me, I have something to do before heading to bed."

"Good night." The couple called after him as he headed in the direction of his bike.

He had to get back into the Natchez Bakery and do some recon while it was closed. Barrett was counting on him for some information.

He may be good at killing the bad guys, but right now, he was just on a recon mission.

CHAPTER 12

*K*illian leaned against the motorcycle and stared at the back door of the Natchez Bakery. The store closed at nine but the employees had been inside until around eleven. There was still one car parked in the back and a light on inside the building.

He crossed his arms and tried to think about anything other than Lilliana. But the image of her beautiful face etched in ecstasy kept flashing in his brain. His body hardened every time he thought about the sounds she made as she'd come in his arms.

The back door opened, and Killian straightened. He kept his position hidden away from the street lights and stepped into the shadows.

A tall, lanky man glanced around before taking a step outside. It was the man who waited on him earlier that day. He tucked his briefcase under his arm and locked the door behind him. He hurried to his car and slid inside. Even from this distance, Killian could hear the distinct click of the car doors locking.

The man pulled away. Killian watched until the red tail-lights disappeared down the street.

"Seemed kind of jumpy for someone leaving work," he muttered to himself.

He shoved off the bike and hurried to the back door. He pulled out a lock picking set and made quick work of the door. He opened the door and stepped inside the bakery. He looked around searching for an alarm but didn't see one.

The building was old, probably on the National Register of Historic Places. Maybe that's why it wasn't wired with an alarm. He made his way back to the industrial kitchen. The stainless-steel appliances, enormous mixing bowls, and a long stainless-steel counter had been cleaned, and all the baking equipment had been put back in its place.

The scent of sugar and cinnamon lingered in the air. It made him think of Lilliana.

He made his way through the kitchen and into the office. An old wooden desk and straight-backed office chair were the only large items in the room. He eased around the desk and sat in the chair. He tried the top drawer only to discover it was locked. He pulled out his lock picking tools and went to work. When the lock finally clicked, he pulled open the drawer.

It was empty except for a key.

"Figures." He sighed and picked it up. He tried the next drawer. Surprisingly enough, it was unlocked.

He pulled out some papers and files and scanned the documents for any suspicious activity. It contained receipts and orders from various customers. He came across several receipts from a repeat customer who ordered the same thing every time.

The customer was listed as Biker Guy. He always paid in cash. And he always ordered the Hummingbird Cake.

"Why would he keep ordering that? It was awful." He

cringed thinking about how the sugar sweet taste had dissolved into something else. Something bitter.

He put the files back and grabbed the key. He walked through the entire store looking for something that the key would unlock.

Thankfully the bakery didn't leave any inside lights on. It made it easier for him to move about without drawing attention from any passing cars.

He stopped at the display cabinet. The cupcakes and cookies were all gone, the shelves wiped clean. But the cake display where he'd gotten the Hummingbird Cake looked like it hadn't been cleaned at all.

He walked behind the counter and slid open the glass. He stuck his finger inside and swiped up some white icing. He lifted it to his mouth to taste and then stopped. A faint bitter smell hit him. He lifted the icing to his nose and inhaled.

He cringed.

It smelled like cleaning product.

"Maybe that's why the cake tasted awful. They didn't clean the shelves, and some cleaning fluid leaked into the cake." He slid the glass back and wiped off the icing on a napkin before tossing it in the garbage can.

He glanced at the time. He thought about taking the key, but he knew the owner would miss it. He still had not found anything amiss so there was no point in keeping it. He headed back to the office and stopped. Movement from outside caught his attention. He pressed his back against the wall and stared out the front window.

A shape walked slowly to the store and then stopped. It was female judging by the curves and the long, dark hair hanging out of the hoodie she wore. She cupped her hand and pressed her face to the window to see inside.

He sucked in a deep breath. Lilliana.

She stood there, silently staring inside at the empty

display cabinets. A sadness swept through her eyes, and she stepped back from the window. She wrapped her arms around herself and dropped her head.

She looked like someone had kicked her puppy.

Killian's heart tugged in his chest.

He watched her slowly walk away.

*H*e hurried to the office and put the key back and shut the drawer. He ran out the back door and quickly locked it before making his way to the front of the Natchez Bakery.

"Lilliana. Wait up." He caught up to her, and she turned.

"What are you doing here? You still following me?" She narrowed her beautiful green eyes at him.

He would take a lifetime of her stares and glares if it meant he could wake up to her every day.

"What? No." He raked his hand through his hair.

"Then what are you doing here at this hour?" She cocked her head, waiting for him to reply.

He grinned and shoved his hands in his jeans pockets. "I could ask the same thing. It's not safe to be out this late."

"Killian, let's be honest. What happened earlier was a mistake." She lifted her chin.

He stepped closer and picked up a lock of her hair. "It certainly didn't feel like a mistake. It felt . . . perfect."

"I'm sure you say that to all the females." She tugged her hair out of his fingers.

His smile dropped.

"I do not." He frowned. He might compliment the ladies but what he felt for her was different. And she was human. It scared him a little.

"Really?" She arched her brow.

He put his hands on his hips and stared. "Tell me something, Lilliana."

"What's that?" She dug around in her purse.

"How is it that you didn't mind our shared intimate moment, but after it was over, you've acted like you couldn't stand me."

She jerked her head up to him. "I don't normally do that." She lowered her voice as if she were afraid someone would hear.

He grinned. "You don't do what? Hate on a stranger? Or wrap your legs around them?"

"You're an asshole." She curled her fingers into fists.

"But I'm a cute asshole, right?" he asked hopefully.

Her mouth dropped open, and then she slammed it shut. She pressed her lips into a straight line and then something odd happened. A laugh bubbled out of her.

He chuckled.

"I'm sorry." She shook her head and pulled a set of keys out of her purse. "I didn't mean to molest you like that in the garden. I guess I needed to let off some steam."

"I'm not complaining. Feel free to release some steam anytime." He looked away. "If we are being honest here, I don't normally do that either. I mean there's usually dinner and drinks and..."

"Technically, you had both." She grinned.

"I guess you're right." She was beautiful, smart, and funny. A combination that was hard to find.

"What about the hating on me?" He looked at her under his lashes.

"Yeah. About that." She shook her head. "I'm sorry. I'm very possessive about my baking and when someone doesn't like my creations, I take it personally." She shrugged. "Not everyone likes Hummingbird Cake."

He froze. "Hummingbird Cake?"

"Yeah. I make and deliver cakes and pies for the Natchez Bakery. The Hummingbird Cake you spit out earlier was mine." She blushed and looked away.

"I thought the bakery made its own baked goods." Unease snaked up his spine.

"They do. The smaller items like cupcakes and cookies. I make bigger items, like cakes and pies. I've only been doing it for them for the past year or so. Just to make some extra money. My mom spent all her retirement to send me to culinary school, and I want to pay her back." She sighed. "I've been out of school for three years now, and I figured that I would be making more money than I am."

"So you made the Hummingbird Cake?" He cocked his head.

"Yes."

"But that's impossible. What I ate tasted bitter. Nothing like your cooking or baking." He shook his head.

"Bitter?" She frowned and slowly shook her head. "But that's impossible. I never put anything bitter in my cake. Especially Hummingbird Cakes. It has cinnamon, sugar, bananas…"

"Maybe the bakery accidently sprayed some product on your cake when they were cleaning the shelves." He shrugged.

"Maybe." But she looked like she didn't believe him. She glanced at the time on her cell phone. "I need to get back. I still have to make cakes for tomorrow. The bakery called me today and doubled their order of the Hummingbird Cakes. It will take me all night." She pushed her hair away from her forehead and looked up at the night sky, a small smile on her face. "You know, I used to love nights like this. Springtime in the air, a new chapter in life, and a night sky decorated with stars and a moon."

He followed her gaze upward. "You know, I could help you out. I'm pretty good in the kitchen." He looked back at her. She blushed.

His body warmed.

"I mean, I know how to do some cooking myself. I can help you bake the cakes," he held up his hands, "but no way can I decorate them. That's not my thing."

"Are you sure you don't have anything else to do tonight?" She frowned and looked around the empty parking lot. "What are you doing out here anyway? Everything in this part of town closes at nine. And there are no bars in this area."

"I was just out for a ride on my bike." He shoved his thumb over his shoulder. "I ended up here."

"So you're the one with the Harley Davidson Breakout at Monmouth. I should have figured." She stuck her hands in her jeans pockets. The spring air skidded between them and lifted a few strands of her hair. Her scent drifted over him, and his body warmed and tightened.

He let out a low growl.

"Are you sure it's safe? Me and you together in the kitchen?"

"I'm going to assume you're asking if we are going to end up with our clothes off." He grinned.

She blushed and looked away.

"Lilliana, I understand that getting those cakes made is very important to you. As much as I want to make love to you, this time without any clothes on, I promise to keep my urges under control in the kitchen." He held out his hand. "I promise."

She nodded and took his hand. "Great. I'll meet you back at the house."

He watched as she got into her car and drove away before heading back to his bike.

This was going to be one long night, trying to keep his mind on cakes and off of the woman he couldn't stop thinking about.

CHAPTER 14

*T*hank God, the kitchen at Monmouth had double ovens. What would have taken her all night to cook and decorate only took Lilliana three hours. While she put the finishing touches on all five cakes, Killian cleaned up the kitchen.

She never thought a guy could be sexy cleaning a kitchen, but Killian was hot as hell.

He was tall and lean with muscles spanning across his magnificent body.

She studied him under her lashes. His muscles flexed as he finished drying a mixing bowl and put it back under the stand.

"I think I've cleaned everything." He looked around, and his gaze landed on her. "Did I miss anything?"

She straightened from icing the last cake and looked around. "No. I think you got it all. Thank you. It's great that you've cleaned up everything. Makes coming in to cook breakfast tomorrow a joy instead of a chore."

"Of course." He shot her another one of his panty-melting grins.

Her stomach warmed, and she looked away before he caught her under his spell again. She needed to focus. Men like Killian never got serious about girls like her.

"It's almost four. Sorry for keeping you up so late."

"I don't mind. I didn't have anything else to do. I'm kind of on vacation." He shrugged.

"So, what is it you do? You know, for a living?" She carefully put the last of the Hummingbird Cakes into the cake box for her delivery tomorrow. "You don't exactly look like the type that usually stays in a plantation bed and breakfast."

"I've been to B&Bs before. In fact, there's a nice one tucked away in the mountains up in Eureka Springs that I am very familiar with." He snorted.

"Really?" She laughed. "Sounds romantic. You must have taken a girlfriend there."

"Nope. I was with Brutus and…." His voice trailed off.

She turned and looked at him. "Brutus? I'm guessing that's not a female." Shit. Had she pegged him wrong? What about the crazy kissing and rubbing against each other like cats in heat?

"It's not like that. Brutus is like a brother to me." He shook his head and studied the ground. "It was a business trip."

"What kind of business are you in?" She relaxed and gave him a grin. "You know, Mrs. Spell keeps telling everyone you are a famous rock star."

He grimaced. "I know. I should have corrected her, but I kind of like it."

"You like being someone else for a change?"

"Yeah." He grinned.

"I wish I could be someone else." She sighed.

"Why would you want to be someone else? I mean you're living your dream. You are getting rave reviews with the dinner guests at Monmouth, and you are killing it at the Natchez Bakery." He frowned.

"Not exactly." She took a deep breath and then let it out. "The Natchez Bakery doesn't credit me with my own cakes. They said they don't want the customers knowing they are selling creations from outside their own kitchen."

"That doesn't make sense. As long as they're selling who cares if it doesn't come from the bakery?" Killian shook his head.

"I even told them I would be willing to quit working here and come to work full time at the bakery." She shrugged. "But they said they didn't need anyone full time. They want my cakes but not me."

"That's bullshit." Killian growled. "And you don't want to stop selling them cakes because you need the money to pay your mom back."

"Right. He even went as far as giving me a raise. The money is good. I can't turn that down just because of my pride." She lined up the cake boxes in a perfect row. "It's not a big loss or anything. I mean I still get to make cakes and do what I love. For that, I'm grateful."

"It's not fair. Customers should know that you are the one making those cakes." He shook his head and paced.

"Life is not fair." She reached out and touched his arm. "I'll get my chance; it will just have to take a while longer."

He turned and looked into her eyes. "You shouldn't have to wait for what you really want." He reached down and caressed her cheek.

Her heart somersaulted in her chest. Her lips parted, and she sucked in a gasp at the electric thrum of his touch. Suddenly all thoughts of dreams and goals vanished into nothingness. All that was left was her desire for him.

He bent his head and kissed her. The gentle move of his lips across hers quickly turned demanding. She opened her mouth, giving him permission to deepen the kiss.

Her hands slid up his arms and entwined in his long hair. She broke the kiss and stared up into his dark eyes.

"I don't want to wait." She grabbed his hand and led him out the back door and into the night.

CHAPTER 15

Killian's heart thrummed in his chest. He let Lilliana lead him to a small, white cabin behind the mansion.

She stopped at the front door and dug in her pocket to retrieve a key. He held out his hand.

"I don't usually take strangers back to my bed." She placed the key in the palm of his hand.

He smiled. "I'm not a stranger. We've already been…acquainted."

He shoved the key into the door knob and turned. The tumblers clicked into place. He opened the door and stepped back, allowing her to enter first.

He shut the door behind them and reached for the light switch.

"No. No lights," she said in the dark.

"But I want to see you." He frowned. He wanted to see every inch of her incredible beauty so he could take it with him for the rest of his life.

"You will," she whispered and flicked a lighter. She went around the small space lighting candles on the bedside table, the counter of the kitchenette, and along the mantle of the small fireplace.

He looked around the room. The walls were white shiplap. The hardwood floors were original, and judging by the scrapes, had seen a lot of life. The rice bed was antique and adorned with a fluffy, white comforter and gray pillows. The kitchenette had a small refrigerator, hot plate, and an expensive coffee pot. The fireplace was original to the building and looked to still be functioning. The small door along the wall led to a small bathroom. A large chair sat near the wavy panes of a window that overlooked the garden. Painted art pieces hung on the walls, giving the otherwise white space some color.

It was uncluttered yet cozy.

Killian came up behind Lilliana and wrapped his arms around her waist. She sighed and leaned against him.

He buried his face into the sweet spot on her neck. She grabbed his hands and led his palms up her stomach to cup her firm breasts.

He rocked his erection into her bottom. His thumbs rubbed small circles across her bra-clad nipples. His mouth watered to taste them. He knew she was as sweet as she smelled.

She turned in his arms and under the soft glow of candle-light, she looked like a fucking angel.

His angel.

"I want to taste every inch of you.' His voice was harsh as the words spilled out.

Her lips parted, and he didn't waste any time in covering her lips with his.

Her hot tongue slid against his and when she sucked on his tongue, he growled.

His human was playing with fire.

He broke the kiss and tugged her shirt over her head. His

53

gaze soaked in her pink bra and hard nipples straining for his touch. His fingers made quick work of the button and zipper on her jeans. In a flash, they were down her hips and on the floor.

"You too," she demanded as her fingers shoved his jacket off his shoulders, and she tugged at his T-shirt.

He grinned and gently pushed her hands away. He tugged the shirt over his head and let it join her jeans on the floor. When she reached for his zipper, he didn't stop her. He watched as she undid his jeans and shoved them down.

She blushed when his erection sprang out.

"I don't like wearing underwear." He shrugged.

She grinned and took him into her palm. "Good. That makes this easier." She slid to her knees in front of him and took his entire length into her mouth.

CHAPTER 16

*L*illiana teased Killian with her tongue, keeping her gaze locked on his.

He was impressively large, not that she'd been with a whole lot of men. Desire pooled low in her stomach, imagining what he was going to feel like inside her.

"Easy. Make this last." His voice was gruff and commanding, and it turned her on even more.

"Like that, do you?" She licked the side of his thick cock and slid her hand up and down his thick length.

"Yes." He tightened his hand in her hair.

She sucked him deep into her mouth, savoring the taste of his male arousal.

"Enough." He moved away and helped her to her feet. "It's my turn to taste you." His mouth came down on hers. She moaned under the delicious assault of his kiss.

His hands found the clasp on her bra, and he made quick work of undressing her. His large hands moved to the sides of her panties. He stuck his thumbs on either side of her hips and tugged the lacy material down to the floor. He deftly picked her up in his muscled arms and walked over to the bed where he gently laid her.

He crawled between her legs, a lion stalking his prey. He shot her one last panty-melting grin and buried his face between her thighs.

"Oh, God." She arched against his face as his tongue found her wet center. His tongue was slow, deliberate, and thorough.

"You taste better than any cake I've ever eaten." He grunted. He licked and sucked at her pussy, groaning in delight at his meal.

"Killian." She breathed out his name as pleasure built between her legs. Her orgasm crashed over her like a tidal wave until she was convulsing and digging her nails into his head.

When her body finished shuddering, Killian crawled up and positioned his cock at her heated entrance. She cradled his face between her hands and pulled him down for a kiss.

"You have a condom right?"

He frowned. "A condom?"

"Yes." As much as she wanted him, she was not ready to be a mother. She reached over and dug around in the nightstand drawer. She pulled out a box of unopened condoms and handed him one.

He sighed and obediently rolled the condom onto his erection. He brushed the hair out of her face and kissed her.

She tasted her pleasure on his tongue, and she pulled him close.

"You're so fucking beautiful." He looked into her eyes. Something tugged in her chest, and she tried to convince herself it was just physical pleasure they were sharing.

But she wasn't stupid.

She knew better.

She was beginning to care for Killian.

He slid inside her body, and she shuddered in pleasure. "You feel so good," he whispered. "You feel perfect."

She wrapped her arms around his broad shoulders and held him as he slid his body rhythmically against hers.

She arched up to meet him, thrust for thrust. They moved together against their sweat-covered bodies, each struggling to keep it going longer and not give in to their pleasure.

She wanted this to last. She needed it to last.

She wanted to remember each moment with him so she could recall in her old age how she'd lost her heart to a stranger.

"Lilliana." He looked into her eyes. She shuddered as another orgasm rolled over her. He held her close and found his own release. He spilled his seed deep inside her.

He rolled over and pulled her into his chest. They spent several minutes like that. Touching and feeling and saying all the words, without anything spoken.

CHAPTER 17

*K*illian woke up to the sun crawling in the window of a tiny cabin. He frowned and then smiled as he remembered where he was.

He'd spent the night with Lilliana. In her bed. In her body.

A slow, satisfied smile settled on his lips, and he rolled over to pull her into his chest. He froze. The bed was empty.

A note with his name sat propped up against the pillow.

He sat up and picked up the paper.

Killian, I had to go make breakfast for the guests at Monmouth. Then I have to make my cake deliveries. I left you some cinnamon rolls by the coffee pot.

Xoxo

Lilliana.

XOXO? Did that mean she loved him? Or did it mean just hugs and kisses? Was it a generic greeting or was she trying to say she felt something more?

"Ugh. Stop being a pussy, Killian." He slung off the covers and grabbed his jeans from the floor. After sticking his feet in and pulling them up, he didn't bother to zip them.

He walked over to the fresh pot of coffee and smiled at the large plate of sugary goodness waiting on him.

"Sex and sugar. Two things I love the most." He cheerfully poured himself a cup and grabbed the plate. He headed over to the overstuffed chair, sat down, and proceeded to devour the cinnamon rolls.

He glanced at the alarm clock on the bedside table. It was almost nine o'clock. He didn't usually sleep in, but he'd had sex until the sun was starting to peek over the horizon.

He grinned as he thought about last night.

Lilliana had been just as beautiful and sexy as he imagined. She'd seemed to be in sync with what he wanted. She did everything that turned him on and more. He'd known by the number of orgasms he'd given her that he'd satisfied her as well. As a Were he didn't normally wear a condom since it was impossible to for him to impregnant a human nor did Weres carry sexually transmitted diseases. But last night he didn't mind. As long as he could have her.

He set the empty plate down and picked up his coffee cup. He deeply inhaled the scent of chicory and looked out the window.

The garden was empty, and the only movement he saw outside was the mallard ducks and Canada geese walking toward the small pond, probably looking for some food.

Monmouth was certainly beautiful. It was the perfect romantic getaway or honeymoon spot.

He rubbed his hand across his chin. Had Lilliana already left to deliver her cakes? He knew that breakfast would be over by now. She probably left as soon as she was done cooking so she could get her cakes delivered.

He'd watched her make the cakes last night and had even taken the liberty of tasting the batter. It tasted wonderful. No bitterness whatsoever.

He was convinced. The bakery had mistakenly put some

cleaner near the cake, and that's what had made it taste so bad.

He grabbed his coffee cup washed it out in the sink. Since he was technically still doing recon on the Natchez Bakery, he was going to grab a shower and head back down there.

CHAPTER 18

"*I* think this is too much money." Lilliana frowned at the wad of cash stuffed in the white envelope. She ran her thumb across the large bills and recounted it again.

"That's a first. A woman not liking money." Emmett sniffed and shoved his glasses up on his rather large nose.

She gritted her teeth and stared. "It's not about not liking money. I like money just fine. This is about you overpaying me. You already gave me a raise, and this," she shook the envelope at him, "is almost four times what I normally get."

"Yes, well." He stood from his desk and went to the door. He poked his head out and shut the door.

Unease crawled up her spine.

She didn't like the vibe he was giving her. She stood and turned to face him. "What are you doing?

He swallowed nervously and took his seat.

"It's more money this week because I need more Hummingbird Cakes."

"How many more?" She preferred standing.

"I need about twenty. Every day."

"Twenty? I can't do twenty cakes a day and decorate them and cook at Monmouth." She gave him an incredible look.

"What if you didn't decorate them? I mean we could decorate them here. It's just frosting." He shrugged.

She cringed. "It's not just frosting." And they were more than just assembly line cakes. They were her own creation.

"Lilliana. The amount you are holding in your hand is the amount of money you would get paid every single day. You take that into account before your artist's heart gets in the way of common sense."

"Every day?" She felt her eyes widen.

"Yes. Every day." He smirked.

She glanced down at the envelope. If she could produce that many cakes every day for a couple of months, she could have enough money to pay her mother back once and for all. Hell, she might even have enough to start her own small business and start her own bakery.

"What do you say?"

"Fine. I'll do it." She nodded her head. "But if I'm baking twenty cakes a day, I'm going to need to see the recipe for the frosting you are going to be using."

"Fine." He shook his head and went to the door. "I'll be right back with the recipe."

She walked around and sat in her chair. She stared at the money in her hand.

Her mind was screaming that this was easy money. But then she reminded herself that there was no such thing as easy money. Baking twenty cakes a day was going to seriously take over her life. From dawn to midnight, whenever she wasn't cooking for Monmouth, she was going to have to be in the kitchen, baking her cakes. She pulled a piece of paper off Emmett's notepad and scribbled down the amount of ingredients she was going to need to produce cakes for the rest of the week.

"Here we go." Mr. Reece held out a recipe card that had seen better days. It was discolored from age and splattered with what looked like melted butter and powdered sugar.

"It's a cream cheese recipe," she said.

"Exactly what you use on your Hummingbird Cakes." He crossed his arms and smirked.

"Yeah. It is." She stood and gathered her purse.

"So, do we have a deal?" he asked.

"Twenty cakes a day is a crazy amount. And to be honest I don't really see that many people in the bakery." She looked at the ground.

"That's because all our customers usually come in before lunch." He cocked his head. "Not to mention we are now doing a great deal of catering for businesses. So we've had quite a lot of deliveries. And your Hummingbird Cake is the most requested dessert we get." He shrugged. "Lilliana, I am no fool. Your cakes are making me a lot of money. I'm willing to pay money to keep the money and the business coming in. Besides, I'm not getting any younger. I will be selling the bakery in another three years or so. And I would like to see someone with talent and enthusiasm for baking buy it." He arched his brow.

She jerked her head up. "Really? But I thought you were barely holding on…."

"Yes, well, businesses go through feast and famine times. Right now, it's feast. And I'm taking advantage of your baking skills." He held out his hand. "I tell you what, I'll give you Saturday and Sunday off. Just bake the cakes Monday through Friday. What do you say?"

She stared at his hand. The urge to shake it was overwhelming. She'd struggled all her life. While other people seemed to always get what they wanted with ease, she didn't. Everything for her was a battle.

Maybe, just maybe, karma was looking out for her.

She took a deep breath and took Mr. Emmett Reece's hand. His skin felt ice-cold against hers, and she had to remind herself that it was because he was so thin. And not her instinct telling her there was more to this contract.

"Emmett, it looks like you have a deal. With Saturday and Sundays off." She looked him in the eye.

"Fine, fine." He looked quite pleased with himself and opened the door for her. "Remember, don't bother doing the frosting; we'll handle that here."

"I got it," she muttered under her breath. She stepped out of the office and down the corridor. She usually came and left through the back door. But today, she changed direction and headed into the bakery.

There were only a couple of people milling about the glass displays. One was an elderly woman clutching a large, black purse. The other was a big, burly man wearing a plaid lumberjack shirt and worn jeans. He had a scruffy red beard, and he looked dirty.

But it was his smell that hit Lilliana.

She cringed and stepped back. He smelled to high heaven.

She watched as one of the employees stepped up to the counter to wait on him, completely ignoring the old woman.

She stepped back and pretended to look at the cupcakes.

"I pay good money to be waited on, and that guy gets attention instead of me." The old woman pulled out a lace handkerchief and held it up to her nose. "And his smell. Good Lord."

"Maybe they are waiting on him so he'll leave faster." Lilliana shrugged.

"Well, this is not the first time that I've been passed over for some smelly man." She shot Lilliana a look. "I'm about to take my business somewhere else."

"What is it that keeps you coming back?" Lilliana smiled broadly at the woman. "Is it the Hummingbird Cake?"

"That?" The woman's eyes narrowed in slits. "They won't sell me a sliver of a slice. They always say that it's preordered by some business. Makes me so mad I could spit."

"You've never had it? I hear it's really good." Lilliana looked at the woman under her lashes.

"Must be. But I'll never know." The woman crossed her arms.

Lillian smiled to herself. "I'm Lilliana." She held out her hand. The old woman took it and forced a smile. "I'm Edith." She looked Lilliana up and down and nodded. "Lilliana, I like that. It's a good, solid name. An older name. Not the latest fad. You should thank your mother for her wisdom in naming you something that means something. Lilliana is Latin, and it means Lily. The flower is a symbol of innocence and purity as well as beauty." Edith nodded. "Your mother was a smart cookie."

Lilliana grinned wide. "I think so too. She raised me herself."

"Oh. No father in the picture?" Edith shook her head.

"He died when I was young. She said he was the love of her life. She never married again."

"Smart woman. One man is enough." She patted Lilliana's hand. "I should know. I've been married five times." She narrowed her eyes.

"Five?"

"Yep, and the only one that was worth a flip was the first one. I should have held on tighter to him. Instead, my pride got in the way." She fussed with her purse and drew her gaze away.

"How do you mean?" Lilliana studied her new friend. There was a sadness in the old woman's eyes that tugged at Lilliana's heart.

"Well, you see, I thought he was not paying me enough attention. I was jealous of his work. He traveled a lot, and I was worried he was with another woman." She shook her gray head. "I let my mind get the best of me. And my pride. One night he came home after a long week of traveling for work, and I started a fight." She wiped at her eyes. "I didn't know any better. I was young and insecure. I threw him out that night, and we were divorced a year later." She looked at Lilliana with determination set in her gray eyes. "Let this be a lesson to you, honey. If you find love, you hold on to it with both hands until your hands bleed. Don't let go. Not even for a second. Because things change at a moment's notice."

Lilliana reached out and touched the woman's wrinkled arm. "I'm sorry." It was all the words she could offer.

Edith smiled and patted Lilliana's hand. "It's all water under the bridge now. I've learned to live in the present. I've buried three husbands, and I've raised a family. I've seen good times, and I've seen bad. I'm a very old woman, and my beauty has faded. But this I know. A good man's heart is hard to find." She nodded.

"You said you buried three husbands." Lillian looked at the woman. "Is your first husband still alive?"

A slight smile crossed the woman's mouth. "How did you know?"

"Because there is still life in you."

The woman jerked her gaze to her, and her eyes widened as if Lilliana had discovered her secrets.

"And since there is life in you, you should make it your mission to go live it." Lilliana lifted her chin.

The old woman's chin quivered. "What if he's dead or worse?"

"Happily married?" She arched her brow.

Edith nodded.

"What if he's neither dead nor happy? What if he is living with regret and thinking of you every single day? Life is too short to be bogged down with what ifs."

"You're right." Edith narrowed her gaze. "What makes you such an expert at such a young age? You're not even thirty."

"No, I'm not. But being raised by a single mom, I've had to grow up fast. And I was lucky enough to grow up with a lot of love. Even if we didn't have much else." Something inside Lilliana warmed and gave her hope.

"You know what, my dear?" Edith gave her a wink. "You are going to find love. And it's going to hit you hard and fast. You're going to want to build a wall and keep him out. Don't. Don't do it. Love comes once in a lifetime. You grab him and hold on to him with everything inside of you."

Lillian's heart flipped in her chest. She nodded.

"Good. If you do that then you'll do just fine." Edith's smile faded as she glared at the cashier. "I think I'm going to go to the other bakery in town since this one isn't keen on keeping customers."

Edith hiked her purse on her shoulder and lifted her chin in the air as she headed for the front door.

Lilliana watched Edith's retreating back. She was more focused on the old woman's words of wisdom than the Natchez Bakery's customer service.

CHAPTER 19

*K*illian frowned at his ringing cell phone.
Barrett.

"Hello?" Killian killed the engine and threw the kickstand on his Harley Davidson. He had arrived at the Natchez Bakery just in time to see Lilliana leave out the front door.

He was going to catch up with her until Barrett rang.

"Any news?" Barrett's impatient tone forced Killian to concentrate on the mission instead of watching Lilliana leave.

"I broke into the bakery and went through the office. There was nothing unusual. Just paperwork and receipts of customers." He scratched the back of his ear and frowned. "I did find a key that was locked in a drawer, but I could never find out what it went to."

"Not good enough. There's been in increase in meth sales in Mississippi. It's starting to leak over into Louisiana. I don't want that shit in my state."

"Understood." Killian sighed. "I can go back in tonight and do another sweep of the place. There might be something that I missed before."

"You do that. And keep me updated." Barrett hung up.

"Not much for words I see." Killian spoke to the phone in his hand. He climbed off the bike and studied the big building in front of him.

There was not a lot of traffic coming in and out of the building. And the people he'd seen were an odd collection. They were either old women who looked like they were dressed to go to church, or they were tattooed guys who looked like they'd never stepped foot in a church.

Kind of like him.

He headed toward the bakery. Since he was already here and Lilliana had been long gone, he might as well buy another Hummingbird Cake.

If this one was bad then he was going to have to tell her. He wanted her to be a success and someone getting a cake of hers that had gotten ruined would not do anything for her career.

He opened the front door and stepped inside.

The room was practically empty except for a guy in a leather biker jacket standing in front of the display case. He had dark-black hair and was built like a tank.

He was also eyeing Lilliana's Hummingbird Cake with interest.

Killian strode up beside him and stuck his hands in his jeans pockets. "I was thinking of getting that cake." He nodded toward the display.

The big guy snorted. "Yeah. That's not going to happen. I already bought it."

"Really?" Killian suppressed a grin. "You must have gotten this cake before."

The guy turned toward Killian and narrowed his gaze. "Why would you ask something like that?" His gaze wandered up and down the Were as if he were trying to figure out if Killian had an angle.

"No reason." Killian shrugged. "I had heard those Hummingbird Cakes were good. Thought I'd come in and buy one."

The large guy cocked his head. "No. You don't want those cakes. Not here."

"Why not?" Killian took his hands out of his pockets. "What's wrong with them?" Had the guy heard something?

"You can't get Hummingbird Cakes here because they are all sold out. Months in advance." The guy turned back to the counter and shook his head. "Besides, you look more like a Twinkie Cake kind of guy."

Something about the way the guy carried himself and the way he talked had Killian's instincts going crazy.

He had a feeling they were no longer talking about cakes.

"Well, I heard those Hummingbird Cakes were good, and the best ones are here." He tapped his finger on top of the glass display case. "At the Natchez Bakery."

The guy turned and smirked. He nodded his head. "I see. You must be one of the new guys." He shrugged. "I wasn't told we were going to have new guys help with pickup and distribution."

Killian crossed his arms. Whatever this guy was talking about sounded a whole lot like drug dealing.

"I was hired at the last minute," he lied.

"Not surprised." The guy held out his hand. "I'm John."

Killian accepted it. "Killian." It rolled out easy enough, and he wondered if he should have given an alias. From the scent of the guy, he was human and not a Were. So, he was pretty sure John didn't know who the Louisiana Assassins were.

"I guess Walter hired you since we've had to order more cakes." John nodded at the display.

"Yeah." Killian remembered to keep his expression neutral. "A lot of cakes means a lot more help."

"It means moving more product." John glared. "You'd think they'd have come up with an easier way to move drugs than baking them in cakes."

Killian's stomach tumbled. Baking them in cakes? Fuck. Barrett had been right about the bakery. His mind flashed back to when he had taken a bite of the Hummingbird Cake back at Monmouth.

He'd noticed how bad it had tasted. He'd noticed the dark-yellow discoloration around the part he'd eaten but he'd just chalked it up to the banana that had been baked in. Now thinking back, he wondered if it had been meth.

Lilliana's Hummingbird Cake.

Had she been in on the whole drug ring?

His stomach dipped to his toes, and his head swam.

"I'm glad they hired another guy. A few days ago, we lost a cake when the owner had sold it to an unknown." John shook his head. "That shit could have gone all kinds of sideways. The owner got in quite a lot of trouble for that." John laughed.

The fact that he'd spit it out was why he hadn't gotten sick after eating it.

Being a Were had a multitude of advantages.

"No doubt." Killian narrowed his gaze on the human.

"From here on out, the owner knows to only sell the cakes to me and no one else." John nodded.

"So, did you bring some kind of truck to load this shit up in?"

"Yeah." John dug his keys out of his pocket and threw them at Killian who caught them midair. "It's parked around back. Since we are getting more cakes today, we are just going to start loading them from the back instead of the front. So it won't draw too much attention to what's going on."

"It's the last thing we need." Killian heard a noise from the kitchen and voices raised. One of them was the owner who'd sold him the cake a few days ago. If he found Killian here, he would out him. "I'll head on out to the truck." He ducked out the front door just as the owner came out of the kitchen.

Killian was careful to keep his hands in his pockets and his head down as he walked down the sidewalk and around the building.

He stopped when he saw the white van parked in the back. He slid the key into the door and unlocked the vehicle.

He glanced around before sliding into the driver's seat. The interior was cluttered with fast food burger wrappers on the floor. He cringed as he caught the stale scent of old cigarettes.

A red lighter, some sticks of gum, and a business card sat in the console.

He picked up the card. The Triple X, the strip club in Memphis.

He quickly memorized the card and put it back as the back door of the bakery opened.

John and the owner stood on the stoop and talked animatedly.

Killian spotted a St. Louis Cardinals hat on the passenger seat and tugged it on his head.

He didn't want to take any chances of the owner recognizing him as the guy who'd bought the cake.

"Hey, Killian." John yelled as the owner stepped back inside the building. "Back the truck up and we'll get these cakes loaded."

Killian nodded and started the van. He eased the van into position at the back door and slid out of the driver's seat. He walked to the back of the vehicle and opened the back doors. John rolled a cart on wheels over to the van. Killian scanned the area behind the man, making sure that the owner was still inside.

"Load these cakes while I take the money inside." John reached inside the back of the van and pulled out a big, black backpack. He unzipped the top and showed Killian the stacks of bundled hundred-dollar bills. "It's crazy what people pay for drugs. Me, I prefer Scotch." John grinned and tossed the backpack on his shoulder.

Killian watched John head back inside the Natchez Bakery.

He quickly loaded the cakes into the back of the van and pulled out his cell phone. He snapped a shot of the cakes and stepped back to take a picture of the license plate. He glanced over his shoulder, making sure he was alone before texting the info to Barrett.

His finger froze. He changed his mind and didn't send the information.

He managed to shove the phone back into his jeans pocket when John exited the building.

"You riding back with me?" John asked.

"Not yet. I've got to handle some other business first." He grinned. "Let's just say I've got more than one boss."

"Yeah. You have to in this business." John nodded and slid inside the truck. Killian watched the van drive away, loaded with cakes and drugs. He tossed the baseball cap to the ground.

He made his way back to his Harley and started the engine. He pulled onto the street and headed in the direction of the van. He quickly caught up.

His phone buzzed, and he knew it was Barrett calling him back. But he couldn't answer right now. He had to follow the van to where the drug dealers were distributing the drugs.

Here was his opportunity to prove to Barrett that he wasn't lazy and he was a good member of his Pack. Here was his chance to prove his worth.

Once he had all the answers, he would report back to his Pack Master.

And then deal with Lilliana.

CHAPTER 20

Thankfully, Lilliana didn't have to cook dinner that night. A lot of the guests had checked out, and Mrs. Spell decided that it wasn't enough to warrant cooking a meal for so few.

It worked out perfectly for her. It would actually give her the time to start cooking her cakes for the bakery. She had already purchased all the ingredients she needed so all she had to do was get started.

She grabbed the pink and white striped apron and tied it around her waist. She gathered her long hair in a loose knot at the nape of her neck and then washed her hands. She pulled out all the cake pans she could find and greased them with coconut oil.

She filled the kettle with fresh water and placed it on the stove and turned the heat up. Once she got the first few cakes in the oven and the next batch made, she could enjoy a cup of tea.

She smiled as she got the first few cakes in the oven. She set the timer and went about mixing the next batch.

For the first time in a long time, she felt like she was finally getting ahead of the eight ball, so to speak.

For the first time in a while, she wasn't the one struggling.

Fate had finally smiled down on her, and she knew she was going to make it after all.

* * *

KILLIAN KEPT a safe distance as he followed the white van to a warehouse in the outskirts of Natchez.

The words on the building stated it was a plastic manufacturer but judging by the number of cars in the parking lot, it looked like it was a cover for something else.

He parked away from the building under the cover of trees. He killed the engine and waited.

John slid out of the van and plucked a cigarette out of a pack he had stashed in his shirt pocket. He lit up the stick and leaned against the van as he blew a steam of smoke between his lips.

Another man came out of the back door. When John saw him, he straightened and quickly put the cigarette out.

"Those will kill you," the stranger said.

"So will this job." John shrugged. "I'm taking my chances."

"Get that merchandise moved inside. We only have an hour," the man ordered.

"What about the new guy?" John asked.

"What new guy?"

"Killian. The one who showed up at the Natchez Bakery and helped load the cakes?" John frowned.

The man leaned in and glared. "I didn't hire anyone new."

John's face went pale.

"Did you tell him anything, John?"

"No, I didn't. I swear." John held up his hands.

Killian watched the interaction between the two.

"If you see this guy again, you shoot him. Then call me." He shoved his thumb against his own chest.

John nodded and hurried to open the back door.

Killian watched from his hiding spot as John moved the cakes one by one inside.

HE FELT his phone buzz in his jeans pocket but decided to ignore it. A line of black cars drove into the parking lot, and men in suits, carrying large assault rifles, got out.

Killian pressed his back against the tree. He glanced at his Breakout, thinking he was grateful for the black paint job that made his bike blend into the shadows of the woods.

All the men went inside except for six who stood guard around the back door.

Killian itched to make a move, but he knew he couldn't advance. He had to bide his time and wait. He had to wait until the cover of night to check things out.

By the time everyone left, it was late afternoon. Killian made sure he was alone before getting on his motorcycle and heading back into Natchez.

The cool spring breeze did nothing to cool his anxiety about what he'd learned today.

Lilliana. Was she involved? He couldn't imagine getting drugs inside a cake without the baker knowing about it. He frowned as he slowed his speed in the city limits. The street lights were slowly coming on, and people were starting to head home or head out to eat a nice dinner somewhere.

He watched a young couple holding hands as they walked down the sidewalk together. They were both dressed up, on a date, and clearly in love. The way she looked up at the guy made his heart tug and made him think of Lilliana.

He shook his head and focused on looking ahead. He was here on a job, not looking for a fucking love connection.

When he pulled into the driveway of Monmouth, his stomach clenched. Lilliana's car was parked in the back near the kitchen.

He debated on whether to go find her now or wait until he'd had a shower and time to think. Whatever he did had to be done diplomatically.

If she was involved somehow, he didn't need her tipping off the bakery owner.

He parked his Harley and killed the engine. He grabbed his phone out of his pocket and sent Barrett a quick text that he was gathering information and would be back in touch later.

He'd call his Pack Master later. Once he had some more information on the inside of the warehouse.

He knew he didn't need to update Barrett until he had been inside the building. He needed to know how they were taking the meth out of the cake and how they were transporting it.

Until then, Barrett would just have to wait.

CHAPTER 21

*L*illiana heard the unmistakable growl of Killian's Harley as he pulled into Monmouth. Her heart quickened, and she quickly checked her appearance in the reflection of the microwave glass.

She didn't want to appear too eager. She knew that guys didn't like clingy women. She'd never really had a guy that she liked as much as Killian or that made her body react like he did.

Hell, she didn't even really know the guy.

But something about him was different.

She shook her head and picked up her tea cup. She lifted the delicate china to her lips and took a sip of the English Breakfast she'd made only minutes ago.

She needed to focus on getting these cakes done, not on her raging libido.

"Ugh." She groaned.

"What is it, dear?" Mrs. Spell walked into the kitchen and poured some hot water from the kettle into a cup. She grabbed lemon and cut it in half and squeezed the juice into the water.

Lilliana straightened and forced a smile. "Just ready to be done with all these cakes, that's all."

Mrs. Spell smiled and stirred her lemon water with a spoon. The silver clacked against the side and echoed in the kitchen. "See what being a great baker gets you? It gets you more work." She patted Lilliana on the arm and examined the cakes. "They just smell divine, dear. When are you going to ice them?"

"Once they are all baked and cooled," she lied. She knew what Emmett had said about not icing the cake. Besides, if she iced them all, she would barely have time to sleep and then get back up and do it all over again tomorrow.

For the next few weeks, her life was going to revolve around Hummingbird Cakes.

"That's great." Mrs. Spell nodded and pulled the kitchen curtain back with her finger. "Ohhh, there's Killian. I need to speak with him about not serving dinner tonight." She set her cup down and hurried out of the kitchen.

Lilliana took another sip and tried to quiet her racing heart. She needed to calm down and get a grip. It certainly wasn't like they were dating.

Or even serious about each other.

They'd had one night of amazing sex.

Utterly, enthralling, amazing sex that she could not get out of her mind, and now she was a basket case.

"I knew better." She set her cup down and moaned. She had a life ahead of her, and she needed to focus on that and her career.

She cringed as she heard Mrs. Spell greet Killian in the hallway. She quickly turned her attention to getting the next layer of the Hummingbird Cake out of the oven.

She put on oven mitts and pulled out the two cake pans of light-brown cake.

She smiled as she set the pans on the counter to cool. The scent of sugar, cinnamon, and banana lingered in the air.

It was a happy scent and took her back to her childhood when her mother would bake for every holiday.

"Oh dear." Mrs. Spell walked into the kitchen and shook her head. "Looks like our Killian is in a bad mood."

"Bad mood?" Lilliana jerked her head over to the older woman. "Did he say what's bothering him?"

"Oh no. And I didn't ask. He just kept looking at the kitchen door." Mrs. Spell picked up her cup and sighed. "He's just probably put out because we aren't serving dinner tonight."

"Really?" Her heart fell a little. She felt oddly like she'd let him down. Which was weird. She barely knew him.

Deep inside, she knew that was a lie.

Her body knew his in a way she'd never experienced with any other man.

She held her breath and waited. The thud of his loud biker boots against the hardwood floor alerted her that he was moving...away from the kitchen and upstairs to his room.

Disappointment washed over her.

She shoved an escaped strand of hair behind her ear and took a deep breath. She needed to calm down and focus. Not on disappointing others, not on pleasing a guy, but on her life and future.

She knew in the end that's all that mattered.

CHAPTER 22

*I*t took everything within Killian to walk upstairs past the painted walls and not to go into the kitchen and find Lilliana.

He knew she was in the house.

He'd smelled her feminine scent the second he stepped inside the front door.

His body had hardened immediately. Despite what he learned earlier about drugs in her cakes, he still wanted her.

He shook his head and shoved the key into the door of his room. After locking it behind him, he tugged all his clothes off and walked naked into the bathroom. He turned on the water and didn't bother waiting for it to heat. He stepped under the cool spray and allowed the water to cool his over-heated, lust-driven body.

He was a fucking Assassin. And one small sexy female had managed to make him fall to his knees with just her scent.

Maybe she was some kind of spy. Sent in to occupy his mind and distract him with her gorgeous body.

He scrubbed a hand down his face.

He was fucked.

Completely fucked.

When he finished taking the world's longest shower, he stepped out and wrapped a white towel around his hips. He didn't bother drying off but walked into the bedroom. And froze.

"I need to talk to you." Lilliana stood there with an extra key in her hand. Her eyes widened, and her gaze dipped down to his towel.

His cock hardened at the evident lust in her beautiful, blue eyes.

"Yeah. I was thinking the same thing." He needed to gain control over the situation and over her.

He couldn't go back to Barrett and tell him he was falling for someone who was happily baking meth into bird cakes.

"How did you get another key?" He narrowed his eyes.

"Mrs. Spell keeps a spare of all the rooms. Just in case." She shrugged. "When you didn't come into the kitchen, I was worried about you. Mrs. Spell said you seemed upset that we didn't serve dinner tonight." She shook her head. "I though you understood that I need this job at the bakery. I need the money so I can pay my mom back."

"At what price?" He crossed his arms over his chest and stared. Would she confide in him and tell him the truth, or when faced with the consequences of her action, would she lie?

She flinched as if he had slapped her. "Excuse me? Do you think I should stop building my life and career just because I didn't cook you dinner? Do you know how sexist that sounds?" Her eyes narrowed to slits, and she turned away. "I thought you were different from other guys out there, Killian. I guess I was wrong."

She reached for the door, but he was quicker. He grabbed her elbow.

"Wait. We are not done. And this isn't about some fucking dinner." He spun her around so he could look into her eyes.

"Then what is it about? I did nothing wrong, and you're acting like I committed murder," she ground out between gritted teeth.

Fuck. Even angry, she was pretty.

"Well, that's what drugs do. They kill," he spat out. He wanted her to feel the pain like he was.

"What?" She looked at him like he had grown a third eye. "What the hell are you talking about? I'm talking about you being pissed at me because I didn't cook dinner tonight. What are you talking about?"

He held her in his arms and stared into her eyes.

"You don't know, do you?" He cocked his head. A weight lifted off his heart and fell to the floor. "Thank God, you don't know." He pulled her into his arms and hugged her hard. When he felt her struggling against him, he loosened his hold.

"Wait a minute, Killian. You need to tell me what the hell you are talking about." She stepped out of his arms.

His towel had loosened and when she stepped back, it fell to the floor. Her mouth dropped open, and she turned away, trying to focus her attention out the window.

"What? It's not like you haven't seen it before," he deadpanned.

"I know but I would like to understand what you are talking about before things …."

"Before things get hot and wet?" he answered playfully. God, he wanted her. Right now, up against the wall, he wanted to be inside her tight body.

He shook his head and waved his hand at the chair. "You need to sit for this."

She swallowed and sank into the chair. Her beautiful,

green eyes were wide and serious. He hated that he was having this conversation right now, yet here they were.

He slid on a pair of jeans. "I'm here on business. But not the business you think I'm here for." He took a deep breath and let it out. "I'm here to investigate a crime."

"Are you undercover?" A small smile crept across her face. "I knew you were keeping secrets."

He froze. "You did?"

"Yeah. You certainly don't give much away when talking about your career." She shook her head. "Besides, I saw that weird tattoo on your back. It looks like military or something."

All the Guardians had the same tattoo on their backs. It consisted of large wings spanning the back with eyes looking out from underneath. It symbolized the ever-watching duty of a Guardian who vowed to protect the innocent and uphold the lupine law.

He had that tattoo. What she didn't know was he also had another tattoo. The Assassin's tattoo.

He, Brutus, and Lorcan were the only ones who carried the tat. And they all had it in a place where it wasn't visible. Brutus had his on his hand. It was the reason he wore leather gloves all year round, to conceal it. Lorcan had his on his inner thigh. Lorcan made it a point to always fuck in the dark, so no female could know he was an Assassin.

Killian had his tattoo on his neck. And it was the reason he wore his hair so long, to cover up the identifiable ink of an executioner's sword that dripped blood of the guilty.

Back before there were silver bullets and other advanced weaponry, all Assassins killed by a sword.

Nowadays, they had more options. Never the less, the tattoo stayed the same.

"Don't lie, Killian." She crossed her arms and lifted her chin.

Very slowly he turned his back to her, revealing his Guardian tattoo.

What she didn't know was he was so much more.

He faced her. "I'm not supposed to be going around telling who I am."

"I understand." She took a slow step forward. "Whatever you tell me stays between us. I hope you know that."

He swallowed hard, trying to decide how much to tell her.

"Sit." He motioned at the chair next to the window. She obeyed, and he sat on the edge of the rice bed.

"It's a long story, so I'm going to try to sum it up."

"Okay." She gave him her full attention.

"I was sent here to investigate the Natchez Bakery. There's been some talk about them running drugs through the business."

"What?" Her mouth dropped open, and she placed her hand over her chest.

"I broke into the bakery after it closed. I didn't find anything, but I did find a key that didn't fit any lock there. So I put it back."

"So they're clean." She breathed out a sigh of relief.

"Not exactly." He rubbed the back of his neck. "I came back during the daytime and ended up talking to a guy named John. He mistook me for one of the newly hired men to pick up cakes. Your Hummingbird Cakes to be exact."

"I don't understand."

"It seems that they are putting the drugs into the Hummingbird Cakes and moving them to a warehouse on the outskirts of town. Out in the country."

"But I was told they are selling those cakes to businesses."

"Did Emmett Reece ever give you the names of the clients who are buying your cakes?"

"No, he just said it was businesses that are buying them."

"Right. The drug cartel. Anyway, it adds up because of what happened in the garden when we met."

"When you spit out my cake?" She narrowed her eyes in confusion.

"Yes. They sold me that cake under the assumption I was one of the guys picking up the drug cakes. That's how I ended up with it. I have the same look, build, everything. Anyway, when I tasted your cake, it tasted bitter. When I looked at it, it looked discolored on the inside. I figured it was the fruit. Looking back, I realized the drugs had leeched out of the plastic bag they were in and had gotten into the cake itself."

"Oh, God." She covered her face with her hands. "What if some family had bought those cakes? It would have killed them. I could have killed them."

"No, you wouldn't have. Besides, they are pretty stringent about who buys them. I think I slipped past them because they thought I was a bad guy." He shrugged. He was an Assassin, so he wasn't that far off the mark.

"They are wanting your cakes because they are big and tall enough to move enough product. They are probably cutting a hole in the center and putting the drugs in there."

"I'll have to call Emmett right now and tell him I will not be selling any more cakes to him." She looked up with tears in her eyes. "God, Killian. I'm a mule."

He grinned and went to her. He knelt in front of her. "You, sweetheart, are not a mule. Technically, your cakes are the mules."

She groaned and buried her face into her hands. "Not helping at all."

"Jeez, Sorry." He pulled her hands away from her face and forced her to look into his eyes. "I'm really bad at reassuring women I care about. I've not had much practice."

He didn't tell her that he'd never felt like this with any other female. Just her.

In that moment, he knew his world had changed, shifted into something that would never be the same.

CHAPTER 23

Lilliana's body heated. Her heart clutched.

"Really? I would have thought you've had lots of practice." She reached out and ran gentle fingertips down the side of his face.

"Not really. I've never gotten this close to a female before." He closed his eyes at her

touch.

"Female. Do you call all women female?" She laughed softly.

"Are you offended?"

"I should be. Oddly enough, I'm not."

When he opened them, he placed his hands on the armrests and leaned in. Her heart fluttered.

He pressed his mouth against hers, and immediately she let out a moan.

He always did that. He always managed to pull something out of her soul when he touched her.

Her body warmed under his seductive kiss, and she ran her hands up his arms to his shoulders. She wound her fingertips into his long hair and held him prisoner against her mouth.

He deepened the kiss, their tongues dancing against each other as their bodies rubbed together.

"More," she begged.

He trailed his mouth down the side of her face to her neck. She arched against him, pulling him closer and needing to feel him against every curve of her body.

He pulled back and looked down at her with dark eyes.

He swept his arms under her knees and carried her over to his bed. He placed her gently in the middle. He pulled his shirt off and tossed it on the chair. Next, he rid himself of his jeans.

Her face heated when she saw he wasn't wearing any underwear. And he was already hard for her.

"Your turn." He grinned. He crawled onto the bed, and his deft fingers flew over her zipper. He pushed her jeans down her legs and tossed them on the floor. He crawled between her legs and buried his face in her stomach. He took his time kissing her stomach as he made his way up her chest. He pulled back and pulled her shirt over her head. She lay before him in her black panties and matching bra.

"These are pretty, but they have to go." He kissed her as he made quick work of ridding her of her panties and bra. He lay between her legs, his erection pressing against her stomach.

She cradled his face between her hands and pulled him down for a kiss. His tongue entered her mouth at the same time he entered her between her thighs.

"Killian," she breathed against his mouth. He filled her with pleasure and rocked against her body.

He looked into her eyes with such emotion, it rocked her to her core. Never had she felt such intimacy.

She held on to him, memorizing every muscle in his back

with her fingertips as he moved in and out of her body. She dug her fingernails into his back as pleasure pooled low and then exploded throughout every cell of her body. She arched against him and cried out his name.

He buried his face into her neck and growled low and deep as his own orgasm swept over him.

They stayed like that, connected in body and soul, until every tremor of her body was finished.

Killian rolled off her and pulled her into his arms.

"I wish I could stay, but I have to get back out there. I'm following the truck from Natchez Bakery to the warehouse so I can see where they go next." He kissed her mouth and slid off the bed. He found his jeans and slid them over his hips.

She climbed off the bed and froze. Her face went pale.

"What is it?"

"We didn't use a condom. I've never not used a condom before."

"I don't have anything if that's what you mean." He laughed.

"I'm not talking about that. I'm not on birth control." Her eyes grew wide.

"You don't have to worry about that either."

"Are you...sterile."

He bit his lip and stifled a grin. That wasn't it at all. But he certainly couldn't tell her the truth. That werewolves and humans couldn't conceive a child together.

"Just trust me when I say, you aren't going to get pregnant."

Her slender shoulders relaxed and she looked around for her clothes. Spotting them, she quickly dressed. "I'm going with you."

"Lilliana, I don't think that's a good idea. It's not safe." He scowled.

She shook her head. "It doesn't matter. I'm going, and you're not stopping me. You head down the stairs, and I'll go out the secret back way so I can grab my boots and jacket. I'll meet you at your motorcycle." She gave him a quick kiss and started out the door.

He grabbed her arm. "Wait. There's a secret back way?"

She grinned. "Of course there is. They have them in all the old plantation homes." She winked and headed down the hallway.

CHAPTER 24

Killian hurried down the stairs. He needed to get a move on if he was going to find out where they were taking those cakes after they got to the warehouse.

"Killian! Is there anything I can get you?" Mrs. Spell smiled broadly from the bottom of the stairs.

He repressed a groan. He didn't have time for chit chat. He had Were business to take care of.

"Mrs. Spell." He forced a smile. "No, I'm just headed out."

Her smile faltered. "I'm so sorry we didn't have a dinner prepared for tonight. It's just that we didn't have enough guests to warrant cooking all that food."

"Not at all. In fact, I'm just going out to meet some clients."

"Is that right?" Her ears seemed to perk up. "What kind of clients would that be?"

"Let's just say they're in the music business," he lied. He'd already heard how she thought he was some kind of rock star, so she wouldn't question his answer.

"I see." She nodded eagerly.

"I have to get going."

"Of course. And I'll see you in the morning for breakfast," she said to his retreating back.

"Yes. In the morning," he called over his shoulder.

He hurried through the dark toward his Harley. While he didn't want to take Lilliana with him, he figured she'd find a way to go without him. At least with him, she'd be safe.

He came to a halt when he spotted Lilliana.

She was dressed in black biker boots and a black leather jacket. Her dark hair was down around her shoulders, and she was propped up against his Harley.

She was fucking beautiful.

"Hey," he said and moved toward her.

"I was wondering how much longer you were going to be." She grinned. "Mrs. Spell corner you?"

"How'd you guess?" He slid onto the bike and waited for her. She climbed on behind him and wrapped her arms around his waist.

It felt right, which started to worry him.

Killian started the Harley, and the monster growled to life. He grinned as Lilliana tightened her arms around his waist and rested her head against his back.

It felt right.

A little too perfect.

He pulled out of the driveway of the mansion and onto the street.

Traffic was light. Natchez was a small town; people didn't stay up all night and party.

Completely different than New Orleans where residents never went to bed.

He increased his speed, letting the rumble of the bike soothe his nerves.

He didn't like putting her in danger like this. But there was no way around it now.

The cool air skidded across his skin. The scent of honeysuckle and daffodils collided with the odor of impending danger.

He turned the bike onto the street where the bakery was located and slowed his speed.

He parked away from the street lights a block away. He killed the engine and let her slide off first.

He grabbed her hand, lacing his fingers through hers. "Stay close."

CHAPTER 25

a couple of large guys were milling about the front of the store. Killian recognized one of them as John. He made a change in direction and headed away from the Natchez Bakery.

"What are we doing?" she asked.

"Going the long way."

He kept his steps slow and leisurely. He wrapped his arm around her shoulders and pulled her tight against him. She followed his lead and tightened her arms around his waist and snuggled into his chest.

"See. I know how to look like I'm on a date." She smiled.

His heart tugged. "When this is over, we will go on a real date. I promise." He kissed the top of her head.

He pushed away romantic thoughts and focused on the task at hand.

They made the block and ended up behind the Natchez Bakery. There were two trucks parked there, and two large guys were loading up the cakes in the back, ten in each truck.

They looked around and then slid into the driver's seats of the trucks. They pulled out of the parking lot.

"Come on." He tugged her hand and hurried to his Harley.

He started the engine, and she hopped on behind him. Within seconds, they were dashing down the street, attempting to catch up to the trucks.

CHAPTER 26

Lilliana clung to Killian as they raced down the street. Danger and excitement drifted on the cool air. Killian was an expert driver, forcing the monster of a bike to go where he wanted it to go.

She smiled to herself, despite the danger they were most likely driving straight into. Handsome, dangerous, gentle.

That's how she saw Killian. God, the male had a body that made her mouth water. He knew how to use it to pull every drop of pleasure out of her too.

The moment she first laid eyes on him, she knew there was something dangerous about him. Maybe it was the way he carried himself, slow and deliberate like he was stalking his enemy and making a choice whether he should live or die. She thought it something hidden behind his eyes. Despite the easygoing air he tried to project, there was something behind those gray eyes.

Despite all those things, Killian was gentle. The way he held her when they were making love, and the way he kissed her like she was a treasure, or the way he was always considerate of her feelings. Yes, Killian was gentle indeed.

Her chest tightened. She knew he wasn't going to stay in Natchez forever. She couldn't expect him to. Not here in Natchez, Mississippi with her.

She took a deep breath, tightened her arms around Killian, and didn't bother wiping the tears flowing down her face.

CHAPTER 27

They arrived at the warehouse just as the two trucks were backing into the loading docks.

Killian parked the bike near the tree line under the cover of shadows and away from the warehouse.

Lilliana slid off the bike, and he followed. He pulled her close to his side and watched as the men unloaded the cakes and carried them into the warehouse. They didn't bother putting them in cake boxes.

She pressed a hand to her churning stomach.

She was part of a drug operation now, whether she knew about it or not. If someone realized those were her cakes, her future would be forever ruined.

"We need to wait until the drivers and the trucks leave. Just be patient." He reached for and squeezed her hand.

She took a deep breath and forced herself to watch the criminal activity in front of her.

It didn't take the two men long to unload the cakes. When they were done, they piled into their trucks and left the parking lot.

"Are we going in now?" she whispered in the dark.

"We are not doing anything. Just me. You stay here," Killian commanded.

She narrowed her eyes, about to argue, but a black SUV pulled up to the back of the warehouse.

"Do you know who that is?" she asked.

"Not sure but I'm guessing it's the buyer of all those cakes." Killian cocked his head as he assessed the situation. He looked so serious and intense that it made her blood heat with lust.

She forced her gaze away from him and looked back at the warehouse. Her career was at stake. She needed to focus on that and how to rectify the situation before her future was ruined forever.

The driver of the vehicle got out and opened the back door. A tall man slid out of the car. He was dressed in a suit and tie. He walked toward the back door of the warehouse with a slow, confident stride. Killian couldn't make out his face, only that he had blonde hair.

As soon as the man entered the building, two guards in the vehicle walked in behind him.

"He'll be in there a while." He took a deep breath, debating his next move.

"So shouldn't we get a closer look?" she whispered.

"Let's wait a minute. He's probably waiting on someone else."

"How do you know?"

"I just have a feeling," he whispered back.

"So we just wait?" She sighed. "I thought investigators had exciting jobs" She crossed her arms and stared at him through the dark.

"Yeah. It's either fighting or waiting and observing. You know, feast or famine." He shrugged.

The low rumble of a car had him tensing all his muscles. He watched another vehicle pull up to the back of the warehouse. It was an expensive sports car from the looks of it. Two men, dressed in suits and ties, slid out of the vehicle, took a quick glance around the parking lot to make sure they were not being watched, and headed inside the building.

"Now can we go in?" she asked.

"You are so impatient to rush into danger." He scowled.

"I'm not rushing into danger. I'm rushing into trying to save my career. The quicker we figure out how they are using my cakes and to who they are selling to, the quicker we can stop it." She sighed.

"Lilliana, I know you want to help. And I know you want to save your career. I really don't think that your career is going to be harmed. We will bring these guys to justice, and your name will never be brought up. If anything, it will ruin the Natchez Bakery's rep. I doubt that guy will have a future in the baking business."

"That's sad." She shook her head.

"Don't feel sorry for him. He's using you and your cakes."

"I know. But it's sad for someone to stoop so low. I can't help but feel a little sorry for him."

He pulled her into his arms and looked down at her. "You are amazing, Lilliana Beckway. I've never met a female with a bigger heart."

"Well, don't get me wrong. If I get in a room alone with Emmett Reece, I will give him a piece of my mind. And maybe a punch in the eye." She grinned.

"My little fighter. I like it." He grinned and bent his head. He covered her mouth with his in a gentle kiss. When he forced himself to pull away, he looked down into her glazed eyes.

"No one has ever called me that before," she purred and tightened her arms around his waist. "I like it."

"Good. It fits you." He held her close and looked back at the warehouse.

He needed to get his head right and stop trying to make out with her in the dark.

It was so hard to resist her.

She was his kryptonite.

He finally let her go and focused on what he came there to do. Recon. He waited another good five minutes.

"I don't think anyone else is coming. You stay here, and I'm going to get closer so I can see what they are doing."

"How are you going to see anything? There aren't any windows." She looked up at him.

"I know. I'm going inside." He smirked and took off toward the warehouse.

CHAPTER 28

*L*illiana's mouth dropped when Killian took off toward the warehouse, leaving her alone in the woods.

"He's crazy if he thinks I'm just staying behind," she muttered and ran toward the building.

Killian stopped at the first van. He crouched and pulled something out of his jacket and then put his hand underneath the back bumper. He moved to the other van and repeated the action.

She wondered if he was putting some kind of tracker on the vans. He stood and ran to the back door. He slowly opened the door and eased inside. She skidded to a stop and looked around. She didn't hear any cars coming or see any movement from the shadows. Confident she was alone, she reached for the door and opened it.

She heard faint voices coming from inside. She peeked inside. The hallway was empty. She stepped inside and eased the door behind her so it wouldn't slam shut.

The inside of the building had a weird scent. She

expected it to smell old from being unused. But instead it smelled of cleaning product.

She glanced to her right and her left. She rubbed her hands on her jeans. She had no idea where Killian had gone.

She grimaced and turned to her left. She slowly made her way down the hallway. The voices were becoming more distinct.

She froze when she heard footsteps headed toward her. She glanced to her right. There was a door. She tried the handle. It gave and she hurried inside and quietly shut the door behind her. She pressed her back up against the wall and held her breath. The voices and footsteps grew louder until they echoed in her ears.

She blinked in the dark, letting her eyes adjust and trying to slow her breathing.

"I told you I need more cakes," a male voice said angrily. He had no accent, not even Southern. "How can I move more meth with only twenty cakes a day?"

"I told Reece. He said he was already pushing that female baker to just do twenty. He thinks she will refuse any more orders after that. Plus, he told her she could have Saturday and Sunday off," the second man spoke. His accent was different and sounded more like he was native to the South.

"Saturday and Sunday off? What the hell? It is not up to him to be handing out days off. I'm running a fucking business here not a daycare." The first man hit his hand against the door. She froze.

She held her breath until her lungs ached.

"I get it, Ringo. I get it. Maybe we need to get a different supplier. I mean, why can't we just stuff them in some Twinkies?"

"Twinkies? Do you know how many fucking Twinkies we'd have to fill to move all that meth?" Ringo growled.

"Plus, we have a method and a system that's working. I don't want to fuck that up."

"Fine. I'll get Emmett Reece to persuade the girl to make more cakes." The other man sighed.

She took a small breath and cringed at the cigarette smoke.

Footsteps fell hard on the hallway until she couldn't hear them anymore. She placed her hand on her stomach and calmed her racing heart.

She slowly opened the door and peered out.

"Shit." She covered her mouth and glared at Killian standing in the doorway. He pushed her back inside and shut the door.

"What the hell are you doing here? I told you to stay put," he whispered loudly.

"I know. But I couldn't let you go in by yourself." She shrugged. "Besides, I found out some information."

"What?"

"They are wanting me to make more cakes and not have the weekends off. I get the feeling from these guys that refusing is not an option." She tried to search his face in the dark. "Did you find out anything?"

"I overheard two of the hired guns that they are shipping the cakes to Memphis. I knew that city had drug problems, but I had no idea that Mississippi was responsible for shipping it to them." Killian forked his fingers through his hair. "Barrett is not going to be happy about this shit."

"Who's Barrett?"

"My boss." It wasn't a lie. Just not the full truth.

"I need to find out where in Memphis they are taking the drugs. We know that Natchez Bakery is producing it. And now I need to make sure I find and take out who the buyer is."

"Take out? That doesn't sound very honorable. Aren't you

suppose to arrest them instead of killing them?" She cocked her head.

Killian didn't reply, and suddenly the energy in the room shifted slightly.

"Killian?" She reached out to touch him, but he grabbed her hand.

"We need to get out of here. I wish I could drop you off at Monmouth, but I have to follow the vehicles to Memphis."

"I don't want to be dropped off. I want to come with you."

"And when your cakes aren't delivered tomorrow?"

"It won't matter. We'll have them by then. Besides, I'm never making another delivery to Natchez Bakery again."

CHAPTER 29

Killian opened the door and peered outside. He sniffed the air. The human scent was faint. Good. The men had at least left the hallway.

He held Lilliana's hand and pulled her behind him down the hallway. His ears perked up, alert for any sounds of approaching footsteps.

He didn't like putting her in danger like this. But he had set a course to follow, and he couldn't deviate now. Barrett was depending on him, and he wasn't going to let his Pack Master down.

He smelled the danger before he saw it. His gut clenched. He stilled.

"What is it?" Lilliana whispered a little too loudly.

"What are you two doing here?" A large man with a beard and an assault rifle stepped out from the shadows of a doorway. He aimed the gun right at them.

"We were just looking for a place to party, ya know." Killian gave him a relaxed grin and hoped like hell the man bought the act.

The man narrowed his eyes and looked between him and Lilliana.

"You come all the way out here to party?" His scowl deepened.

"Just be cool, man. Don't be all uptight." Killian laughed and pulled Lilliana into his chest. "Just looking for a quiet place for me and my woman."

Lilliana stiffened under his not-so-respectful term but said nothing.

"Allen, what's the hold up?" Another man stepped out of the door. He stopped short when he saw Killian and Lilliana. His eyes narrowed.

It was the same guy that drove up in the sports car.

"Who the hell are you, and what are you doing in my place of business?" He put his hand in his jacket and pulled out a 9mm pistol.

Killian knew a bullet, other than a silver one, wouldn't kill them. But it would hurt like a mother fucker, and he really wasn't in the mood to deal with a gunshot wound.

"We had no idea this was a private business. We thought it was abandoned. No one's had a business here for…"

"Years." Lilliana filled in his sentence.

"You're lying. People that lie to me get shot." The sports car guy aimed the gun at Killian.

"Well, fuck. It's going to be like that." Killian lost the smile and shoved Lilliana behind him. He lunged for the man. A gunshot rang through the narrow hallway. He felt the bullet whiz past his face as he landed on the guy and knocked him to the ground. He pummeled the guy in the face.

"Killian?" Her voice was different. Off.

His gut clenched. He stopped his assault on the guy and turned.

Lilliana was lying on the ground, her face pale. She held her hand over her heart.

Terror soaked into his bones. He rushed to her side and knelt.

"Let me see," he said gently. He moved her hand out of the way. The two men retreated down the hallway. He didn't know if they were coming back or if they were gone for good. He did know that he had to get them both out of there in case they came back.

Blood seeped through her shirt. He lifted the hem to see the wound. She winced as he moved her arm out of the way.

"Sorry, sweetheart. I need to see."

"I can't believe I've been shot." She sucked in a gasp and closed her eyes.

His gaze landed on the small entrance wound on her arm. His gut clenched and his blood ran cold despite the minimal amount of blood.

"The good news is that it went straight through without hitting anything vital. The bad news is I need to get you out of here before those assholes come back." He looked into her eyes. "Think you can stand?"

"Yeah." She held her breath as Killian helped her to her feet. He listened for approaching footsteps.

"We have to go." He swung her up in his arms and hurried down the hallway in the opposite direction the men had taken off to. He needed to get her somewhere safe before he took those assholes down for good.

He took a left at the end of the corridor. He heard men yelling orders somewhere behind them.

"Hold on, baby." He tried his best to cradle her into his chest and not bump her around as he ran.

"I can take the pain." She spoke through clenched teeth.

It killed him to see her in pain yet trying to be brave. She may be human but she had the heart of a wolf.

He turned down another hallway, putting them farther and farther away from the voices.

He made a right and spotted the door leading out.

"Finally," he whispered and slowed when he reached the door. He tossed one last look over his shoulder before opening the door and hauling ass out into the night.

CHAPTER 30

Lilliana gritted her teeth against the pain in her chest. She was shocked at how fast Killian could run with her in his arms. It was almost like he was super human.

Maybe it was the shock of being shot making her brain turn to mush. Maybe the pain itself was distorting her view of reality.

Killian stopped when he approached his Harley. He gently set her down.

"Can you hold on?" He lifted her up and placed her on the bike.

"I think so." She nodded.

"I need you to do this, Lilliana. Okay?" He eased onto the bike and started the engine.

Voices and men came running out of the building. They were scanning the area and carrying guns.

She tightened her arms around Killian's waist as he peeled out of the tree line. He sped past the men as they shot at them.

She pressed her head against his back and squeezed her

eyes shut. The sound of bullets had a way of making her forget her pain.

Killian increased speed once on the main road. He placed one hand over hers and gave her a reassuring squeeze.

She laced her fingers through Killian's hand. For someone who looked so badass, he certainly was gentle.

She strained her ears, listening for the sound of car engines roaring to catch up with them.

All she heard was the growl of the Harley and the blowing wind as they raced into the night.

She relaxed a little. Pain bit into her chest. She winced and tried to force the pain away.

"Hold on, Lilliana. We will be back at Monmouth soon."

"Monmouth? Aren't we going to the hospital?"

"That's the first place they are going to be looking for us. They are probably already there scouting out the ER. Don't worry. It's not as bad as it feels. It didn't look like it hit any major arteries and the hospital would have just bandaged it up. I can do that."

She nodded against his back and tried to concentrate on anything other than the white-hot pain shooting through her arm.

An eternity later they were pulling into the driveway at Monmouth.

The lights were all off in the mansion and the place was quiet.

Killian drove to her cabin and killed the engine. She tried to get off the bike, but felt nauseated.

"Wait. Let me help." Killian secured the kickstand and eased off the Harley Davidson first. He eased her leg over and helped her off before once again sweeping her up into his strong arms.

"You don't have to carry me. I can walk, you know."

"I'd rather carry you." He hurried to the front door.

"I have the key." She dug into her jeans pocket and produced a key. He held her to the door so she could put it in the doorknob.

She opened the door.

He strode into the dark room and carefully laid her on the bed.

"I'm going to bleed on my comforter," she groused.

"I'll buy you a new one." He countered. He locked the door and went to the bathroom. When he came out, he was carrying some towels and a small first aid kit she kept in the medicine cabinet.

He laid the supplies on the bed and sat. "I need to get these clothes off first." He reached for her jacket.

"You're always trying to undress me," she teased. Thankfully the nausea had eased.

He chortled. "You're not wrong." Sadness crept into his eyes as he removed her jacket. He reached for her shirt. She lifted her hand to his cheek.

"It's okay. Do what you have to. I can take it." She nodded and raised her arms.

Killian quickly pulled her shirt off and tossed the blood-stained garment on the floor.

She gritted her teeth and eased back on the bed. She watched as Killian studied the wound. He lifted his gaze to her. "I need to disinfect it before I bandage it."

She nodded.

He looked around the room. "Do you have some alcohol or something?"

"I have some wine, but I don't think that's going to disinfect the wound."

He got up and went to the kitchenette. He opened the cabinet above the little sink and pulled out a bottle of red.

"The alcohol not for disinfecting. It's for the pain." He

found a corkscrew in the drawer and quickly opened the bottle. He poured a liberal amount into a glass.

He walked over to her and shoved the glass in her hand. "Drink it. All of it."

She winced. "I usually like to savor my nice bottle of Bordeaux. But since this is an emergency, I'll do what the doctor ordered."

She lifted the tumbler to her lips and drank. The tannins of the wine made her wince as she continued to swallow.

When her glass was empty, she shivered and handed the glass back to Killian. "Wine was not made to be sucked down like that. It's almost abusive to the alcohol."

He grinned. "I'll buy you another bottle when you're healed. How's that sound?"

"Sounds wonderful." She sighed as the warming effects of the alcohol seeped into her body.

"This is going to hurt. I'll try to be as quick as I can." Killian's expression twisted in worry and pain.

"I trust you." She gave him an encouraging smile. She did. She trusted him with all her being.

And unfortunately, she trusted him with her heart.

CHAPTER 31

Killian kept his focus as he disinfected the wound. Every time he wiped the blood away, more spilled out. He pressed down on the bullet hole.

Lilliana grimaced.

"Sorry. Just trying to stop the blood." He quickly pressed some gauze to her arm.

"I'm kind of a bleeder. I should have told you that."

"Hemophila?" He frowned.

"No." She forced a smile and shook her head. "No. My mom had me tested once when I was a little girl and it came back negative for that."

"Hold this and I'll give you some more wine." He pressed her hand against the wound and stood.

He grabbed her glass off the bedside table and poured more wine into it.

He wished he had something stronger for himself.

He walked over to the bed and handed her the wine. "Drink this and I'll bandage you up."

She did as he asked and drained the contents of the glass.

She handed him the empty glass back and eased back onto the bed.

She looked up at him with trust in her eyes. It shook him to his core.

He sat on the bed and pulled out some bandages. He pulled the gauze away and applied some antibiotic ointment to the wound. The blood had already stopped flowing.

He wrapped the wound and taped down the bandage.

"You make a pretty hot doctor, Killian," Lilliana said softly. Her words were starting to slur.

He grinned. "Do I now?" He picked up the supplies. He set everything on the bedside table.

"Yes. You do." She poked him in the chest and blinked slowly. "If this investigating thingy doesn't work out, you should totally go into medical school."

"Right. I can totally see myself going to college." He snorted.

"You could. You could do anything. You're really smart." She nodded slowly.

"And you are really drunk." He shook his head.

She frowned. "You don't think you're smart?" She grabbed his arm and forced him to look at her.

He shifted his weight on the bed. "I use my hands and my strength for my job. Not my brains. I was told enough times growing up that I shouldn't aim too high." He forced a laugh.

Old ghosts of insecurity rose up in his mind before he could banish them.

"Your parents told you that?" She frowned.

"My father did. Enough times. My mother didn't really take an interest in me. She was too concerned with her parties and social standing." He shrugged.

"Then they must be eating their words right now. To see how far you've rose."

"I have no idea. I haven't seen them in years."

"What?" Just like that, the frown was back.

"It's easier this way. Besides, the males I work with are my family." That wasn't a lie. Lorcan and Brutus were closer than brothers to him.

"And you have me too." She smiled and reached for his hand. She laced her fingers through his and closed her eyes. "It's funny. You said males instead of men. Like you are talking about animals."

Shit. He needed to watch his language around her.

"Hang on. Let me get you comfortable." He reached down and pulled off her boots. "Jeans too?" He looked at her for permission.

"Yes, please." She smiled sleepily.

He tugged her jeans down past her feet and tossed them on a chair in the corner. He took his boots and shirt off. He left his jeans on and crawled into bed with her and covered her with the throw on the end of the bed.

She smiled and curled her body into his, fitting against him perfectly.

He sighed and let himself drift off to sleep with her at his side and in his heart.

CHAPTER 32

Killian woke before the sun came up. He eased his arm out from under Lilliana's head and grimaced at the soreness in his neck.

He wasn't used to spending the night with a female. He'd always left after sex. With Lilliana, he found himself wanting to linger.

He gazed down at her lying peacefully in the bed. Her dark hair framed around her face, and her long eyelashes rested against her cheek as she lay lost in sleep. He slowly moved the blanket to look at the dressing above her heart.

He gently untapped the bandage and peeked behind it.

The wound still looked angry but it would heal in time. Thankfully the bleeding had stopped.

She blinked and looked up at him with sleepy eyes. "How's it look, Dr. Killian?"

He grinned and trailed a finger down her cheek. "It looks great. Just take it one day at a time."

She smiled wide. "See I told you I could take a bullet."

He lost the smile. "Don't even joke like that."

"Sorry. Just trying to lightened the mood." She eased up into a sitting position and grimaced.

"Wait. Where do you think you're going?"

"I need to get up and cook breakfast for the guests. They're expecting it."

"Oh, hell no. You're doing no such thing."

She frowned. "But Mrs. Spell is expecting it. I've never called in and never miss cooking a meal that I was scheduled to cook."

"Then you are overdue for a break." He pulled back the covers and tucked her legs underneath. "Now you lie here, and I'll make sure she knows you are sick."

"Wait, you can't do that. Why would you be telling her I'm sick? We're not even supposed to really know each other. She's going to think something is going on between us."

His smile widened. "Something is going on between us." He bent down and kissed her lips.

"She doesn't need to know that. She has a strict policy of no cavorting with the guests." She frowned as she shifted her weight in the bed.

"Good. I'm not exactly a guest. I'm undercover. So we can cavort away." He smiled broadly.

"I need to get up." She sat up in bed and grimaced.

"Stop right there. I'm not letting you go anywhere. I'll lock you in this room if I have to." He walked over to the door.

"The door unlocks from the inside, so there's that." She cocked an eyebrow.

He growled. "Look, just don't leave this bed, okay? Can you do that for me?" He turned and stared hard at her.

"Fine. If I get fired, I'll just go to work making donuts for the donut shop down the street." She glared.

"Perfect. I love donuts." He grinned and headed out the door before she could respond.

He strode toward the main house of Monmouth. The light was just turning purple and gray, signaling a start to another day. The air was cool and sharp and felt good against his skin. Despite last night's disastrous recon, he felt hopeful.

Lilliana was okay, and that's all that mattered to him.

He walked up to the back door of Monmouth and opened the door.

Mrs. Spell was standing in the kitchen, making a pot of coffee.

Her eyes lit up when she saw him. "Killian, I didn't expect you to be up this early. The coffee will be ready in a minute."

"Thanks, Mrs. Spell." He rubbed the back of his neck. "I actually was looking for you. Not the coffee."

"Oh, really?" She turned and gave her full attention to him. "What can I do for you, my dear?"

"It's Lilliana. I ran into her outside, and she's really sick. She's not going to be able to make breakfast for the guests this morning or dinner tonight."

Mrs. Spell's brows furrowed. "Oh dear. That's a problem. I've never canceled a meal for my guests before."

"Well, you don't want her cooking. Not with whatever virus she has going on. It could spread to the guests, and they would give you a poor rating on the website."

Mrs. Spell's eyes widened.

"Can't you just cancel?" he implored.

"I'm afraid not. I suppose I can make do this morning with a basic breakfast of eggs, bacon, and toast. But I have no idea what to do about dinner. I already have eight guests confirmed for tonight."

"Just cater it." He shrugged.

Mrs. Spell let out a gasp. Her hand flew to her chest. "Cater it? I could never do that."

"Why not? They are from out of town, they'll never know the difference."

She lifted her chin and pressed her lips into a defiant line. "I would know the difference, Killian."

He fought the urge to roll his eyes. "Fine. I'll cook it."

"You?" She frowned.

"Yes. Me. It can't be that hard." He shrugged. "I've cooked meals before." It was a total and complete lie. He had only grilled a steak or two in his life, but if cooking dinner meant Lilliana had time to recover then he was about to become a top chef.

"I don't know, Killian. Our guests come for an experience. Not some every day meal they can get at home."

"Trust me. it will not be an ordinary meal. Just leave all the details to me." He gave her shoulder a reassuring squeeze. She turned and poured herself a cup of coffee.

"Fine. You cook dinner tonight. But it better not be a bomb. Or Lilliana gets fired." She narrowed her eyes and headed into the sitting room.

He pulled his cell phone out of his jeans pocket and punched in some numbers.

"What do you want?" Brutus growled over the phone.

Killian sighed and swallowed his pride. "I need your help."

CHAPTER 33

"What the fuck is this about?" Brutus scowled and placed his hands on his hips.

Killian clapped him on the back playfully. "Dude, I told you I needed your help."

"You didn't fucking say it was to cook dinner." Brutus growled. "I drove my ass hours to get here because I thought you needed backup." Brutus glared. "Killian, you told me you needed backup."

"I do need backup." Killian shot him a smile. "I need backup in the kitchen."

Brutus glared. "I'm an Assassin, not a pussy foot baker."

"Shush." Killian frowned and pressed his fingers to his lips. "Keep it down. I don't need the whole house to know what we are."

Brutus gave him a bored look. "Killian, how the hell did you get in this position anyway? This has nothing to do with the recon that Barrett sent you on."

"It has everything to do with it." He closed the kitchen door and glared at Brutus. "And if you don't mind, could you keep your voice down?"

Brutus sighed then eased into a chair at the small kitchen table. The wood creaked under his weight. "Fine. But you tell me how me helping you in the kitchen is part of the mission."

Killian rubbed his eyes. "I found the connection between the bakery and the drugs. The Natchez Bakery owner is paying someone to make these big cakes, Hummingbird Cakes, and is using them to transport the drugs."

"Then we need to take down the person baking the cakes and the owner of the bakery." Brutus stood. "Have you told Barrett about this information?"

"No."

Brutus rounded on him. "Why the hell not?"

Killian held out his hand and took a breath. "The female baking the cakes had no idea her cakes were being used for smuggling drugs. She's innocent. And we can't take down the bakery owner just yet because I haven't tracked down where they are transporting the drugs. After dinner tonight, I plan on going back and following them to their destination."

"And tell me again why we are concerned about cooking dinner?"

Killian gritted his teeth. "Because the baker of the cakes is also the cook here at Monmouth. She was with me last night, and she ended up getting shot."

"Fuck, Killian. Are you crazy? Bringing a female with you?" Brutus eyes blazed.

"I had no choice. She's very stubborn for a human," Killian countered.

"A human? Are you fucking insane?"

"Not that I'm aware." Killian shoved his hand through his hair.

A slight sneer tugged at Brutus's mouth. "Now I see."

Killian frowned. "Now you see what?"

"You're not taking this job seriously because you are too busy getting your rocks off with this female human. She must have a golden pussy. You generally prefer to bed female Weres." Brutus snorted.

"Watch how you talk about Lilliana." He growled.

Brutus's eyebrows shot up. "So, her name is Lilliana."

Killian scrubbed a hand down his face. "Brutus, will you stop acting like an asshole and help me with dinner?"

Brutus stared at him in silence. Killian was pretty sure Brutus was going to tell him to fuck off.

"This woman is the one that usually cooks?" Brutus asked.

"Yes. And she needs to keep her job. That's why I told the owner that I would cover dinner."

"Why the fuck didn't you just have it catered?" Brutus glared.

"I told her I would do that, but the owner refused to have something brought in. She says she wants to create a dining sensation for her guests, and they expect a home-cooked meal." Killian forked his fingers through his hair.

"And you called me. Why didn't you call Lorcan? He makes those fancy pants dinners all the time."

Killian studied the floor. "I tried. He wasn't answering his phone."

"So I'm sloppy seconds. I knew you were an asshole." Brutus crossed his arms.

"But you're also a good cook. Remember that meal you cooked for us when we were in the woods tracking down that serial killer? We ran out of food, and you found and killed that squirrel and cooked it over a campfire?" Killian smiled. "That was one of the biggest squirrels I'd ever seen and the tastiest."

"You dumbass. That wasn't a giant squirrel. It was a fucking nutria rat. I swear you can't remember shit." Brutus scowled.

"A rat? Are you sure? It had teeth like a squirrel." Killian suddenly felt a little queasy.

"I know a fucking nutria rat when I see one. I was trying to catch a ground hog, but that sucker was too fast for me." Brutus shrugged. "So I grabbed the rat. Meat is meat."

Killian closed his eyes and took a deep breath.

"Look, we need to cook dinner tonight. I can't do it alone. I need help."

"I'll do it. But after dinner, we are tracking down those drugs." Brutus pointed at Killian. "And don't think your girl-friend is off the hook. I'm going to be doing my own investigation since you're too close to the situation."

"Whatever, man. Just help me get dinner done and out of the way. Where do we start?"

Brutus blinked. "First. We need to get some meat." He gazed out the kitchen window. "I think I know where I can get some." He opened the back door and headed outside.

Killian rushed to the door and poked his head out. "No rats, Brutus. No rats."

CHAPTER 34

Lilliana shifted in the bed. She glanced at the fading daylight and then at the time on her cell phone. It was dinnertime.

Killian had checked on her throughout the day, bringing her something to eat and seeing if she needed anything for pain. She slept on and off for the rest of the day, but now she was itching to get out of bed.

She eased up on her elbows. Her arm was sore but not no longer felt like it was on fire. She pulled back her sleeve and slowly peeled back the bandage that Killian had so carefully applied.

It wasn't bleeding. Lucky for her Killian was right. He knew enough about gunshot wounds to take care of her without taking her to the ER. When he had first suggested it, she'd been shocked. And scared. Didn't he realize she wasn't invincible? But he'd been so convincing she'd given in and let her take her back to Monmouth instead of the hospital.

She threw back the covers and stood.

Her stomach growled. Suddenly, she was ravenous.

She slowly dressed. She would head on to the house and

see what kind of meal Killian had prepared for tonight's guests. And maybe get some for herself.

* * *

After a quick shower, Lilliana put on some jeans and a long-sleeved, red T-shirt. She tugged on her boots and grabbed her keys off the counter.

After locking the door behind her, she made her way toward the house.

The cool night air played with her hair and tickled her face.

She loved spring. It always made her think of new beginnings and that anything was possible. And now, since meeting Killian, it made her think of something she'd never allowed her to fantasize about. Love.

She stopped in her tracks as the "L" word popped into her head.

She shook her head and curled her fingers into fists at her sides.

"No. Don't even put that in your head, girl. He's not the one for you. He's someone important. He has a demanding career, and he's not the kind of guy to settle down." She groaned. Not only had she developed feelings for Killian, she was losing it and talking to herself as well.

"Perfect," she muttered to the night.

"What's perfect?" a deep male voice asked.

She jumped and turned. "Damn, you scared me." She pressed her hand to her heart.

"Didn't mean to. Was just getting some air after dinner." The large male stepped into the light near the back door.

Her stomach dropped. He looked deadly.

She let her gaze drift down his large body. He was the

same height as Killian, just a little stockier where Killian was lean and muscular.

This stranger had a military style haircut, and his eyes were dark brown. He wore a black T-shirt, dark jeans, motorcycle boots, and fingerless leather gloves.

Yet he had the same look behind his eyes as Killian. A look that he'd seen much more than she could imagine.

"Are you one of the guests for dinner? You must have arrived today," she said.

"No and yes." He took his assessing gaze off her and stared out toward the gardens.

"Excuse me?" She blinked.

"No. I was not one of the guests. Yes, I arrived today. I'm Brutus." He looked back at her and scowled. "Killian called me. Said he needed some help in the kitchen."

"I'm Lilliana." She blinked. "You're a chef?" He looked more like a good-looking serial killer to her.

"Something like that. I hear you bake cakes." He lifted his chin and narrowed his cold eyes.

"Killian has been talking about me to you." Her heart fluttered. She didn't know if this was good or bad.

The back door opened, and Killian stepped out into the night. He stopped short when he saw her talking to Brutus.

"Lilliana. You should be in bed." Killian's face creased with concern.

"I actually feel a lot better." She looked from him to Brutus and then back at him. "Let's say there are no residual effects of my illness."

"You mean the gunshot wound." Brutus said.

Her eyes widened.

"It's okay. He knows. He's in the same line of work as me." He lowered his voice as he spoke.

"Oh, so you're a…"

"Yes. He's an investigator too." Killian added. He gave Brutus an odd look.

"Well, here you both are." Mrs. Spell stepped out from the back door of the kitchen. "I was wondering where you two had gone off too." She lifted her chin when she spotted Lilliana. "Lilliana. You seem to be doing better."

"I am." She smiled. "I guess just some rest was all I needed."

Mrs. Spell gave her a nod. "Well, I have to say you need to thank Killian and Brutus. They cooked an amazing meal that had all the guests raving."

"Really?" She looked at Killian who studied the night sky with a grimace.

"Why, yes. They are saying the meal was extraordinary. Our guests from France said they had never had anything tastier." Mrs. Spell smiled at Killian and Brutus. "Well, I have to get back in to serve the sherry in the library. And Killian, thank you so much for your help tonight."

"Anytime." Killian nodded and looked back at Brutus. His expression shifted into annoyance.

"What's going on?" she asked.

Killian stared hard at Brutus. "Dude, I can't believe you served that to those people. That was supposed to be a fancy dinner."

Brutus seemed unbothered. "They all said it was quite tasty."

"They said it tasted like pork." Killian gritted his teeth.

"Or brisket." Brutus added. "That old lady with the blue hair said it tasted like brisket."

"What did you guys cook?" She crossed her arms and studied the interaction between the two males. She could feel the irritation coming off Killian in waves.

Brutus jerked his head toward the direction of the

wooded area behind the house. He squinted. "Did you see that?"

"See what?" The hair on the back of her neck stood at attention. Had those men who had shot her finally tracked her down to Monmouth? Were they coming to finish the job?

"Looks like a possum." Without saying another word, Brutus jogged toward the tree line.

"What was that about?" Lillian blew out the breath she'd been holding.

"That's typical Brutus." Killian shook his head.

"You still haven't told me what you guys cooked for dinner."

He took a deep breath and sighed. "We cooked a stew. Kind of."

"What do you mean kind of? And where did you get the meat? There was a roast in the freezer, did you use that?"

"Not exactly." Killian cringed. "Our meat was fresh."

She narrowed her eyes. Suddenly, she didn't really want to know anymore. Yet she had to ask.

"And?"

He turned toward her. "Brutus killed a beaver and put it in a stew."

"What?" She blinked.

"A beaver." Killian groaned. "I didn't realize that's what he had used until it was too late."

"How did you not know he was cooking a beaver? I mean, is that even safe? It didn't have rabies, did it? Do beavers carry rabies?" Her heart sunk to her stomach.

"I don't know. I don't think so." Killian frowned.

"Does Mrs. Spell know?"

"Absolutely not. She asked what the meat was in the stew. I told her it was an old family recipe." Killian shook his head.

"I can't believe you served beaver meat to the guests." She shook her head.

"Well, the guy can cook. He served up something while we were camping. I thought it was squirrel meat. It was really good. "

"So he cooked squirrels? That's not so unusual. I've heard of people eating squirrel meat in soups."

"Turns out it wasn't squirrel." He cringed. "It was nutria rat."

She pressed her hand to her stomach. "You ate a rat."

"Under false pretenses. In all honesty, I thought I was eating squirrel meat."

"That must have been a really large squirrel."

"Yeah." Killian cringed. "The size should have tipped me off."

CHAPTER 35

"I can't believe you told the female you were an investigator." Brutus glared at him.

Despite the darkness, Killian could see the anger in the Assassin's gaze. "It's better than telling her I was werewolf Assassin." Killian sighed heavily and propped his hands on his hips.

When Lilliana went inside to talk to Mrs. Spell, he had gone after Brutus.

"Did you catch your possum? What were you going to do with it anyway?"

"I was going to make breakfast with it. I make a mean possum sausage. And no, I didn't get him. He ran off when he saw me stalking him." Brutus's glare intensified. "And stop deflecting the conversation. We are talking about Lilliana. You are one step away from spilling the beans about our kind. You haven't been shifting have you?"

"Hell no. Look, she kind of figured out I was here on business. I just went along with it." He shrugged. "She saw my back tattoo and thought it was something to do with the military."

"And we also carry our Assassin mark as well." Brutus held his gloved hand up to Killian's face.

"She's not seen it." Killian lifted his chin. "I made sure of that. When I had her on my Harley, I made sure to wear a gator around my neck so she wouldn't see my Assassin's tattoo. Not that she would even know what that is." He scrubbed his hand across his face. "I'm not an idiot, Brutus."

"Make sure you keep her away from the truth, Killian. You don't want to give Barrett a reason to fire you." Brutus shook his head.

"Thanks for your help tonight," Killian ground out.

"You suck at gratitude, Killian."

Killian frowned. "I'm still shocked you served the guests beaver."

"Stop being a pussy." A ghost of a smile settled on his lips. "Besides, real men eat beaver."

Killian chortled. It was hard staying mad at either of his Assassin brothers.

"So what's the plan?" Brutus crossed his arms over his massive chest.

"I managed to put a tracker on one of the vans last night before I went inside the warehouse." He pulled out his cell phone. "When they start moving, I plan on following them all the way to Memphis and wherever their destination is."

"Great. When do we go?" Lilliana stepped out from the dark.

They both spun around and looked at her.

"You're not going." Killian took a step closer. "You were shot last night. There is no way you're going back."

He inhaled deep. Her scent was the same but there was a slight difference. Something that made him want to pull her clothes off and fuck her in front of Brutus.

"I'm going with Killian. He'll have more than enough backup." Brutus grunted.

"I'm all better. I can go too." Lilliana crossed her arms and lifted her chin. Her beautiful eyes narrowed on him.

He scrubbed his hand down his face and tried to focus on something other than having public sex with her. He shook his head. "I'm sorry. But you are not going. Just me and Brutus. Besides, you need to get those cakes made for the Natchez Bakery so he won't be suspicious."

She opened her mouth, and he figured she was going to argue with him. She lowered her hands to her sides and curled them into fists. "Fine."

His stomach fell. Anytime a female said the word fine, she was anything but.

He was officially in dangerous territory.

"Lilliana…" He reached for her, but she stepped back.

"I have to go. I need to start baking for tomorrow." She spun on her heel and stormed back to the house.

Brutus let out a laugh.

Killian rounded on him and shot him daggers with his eyes.

"Looks like you won't be getting any for a while." Brutus slapped him on the back and headed toward his Harley Davidson Breakout.

"Fuck." Killian growled and looked at the mansion that Lilliana had disappeared into.

Lilliana was hurt and mad, and he was going to have to make it up to her somehow.

Right now, he had a mission to complete.

CHAPTER 36

Lilliana cringed at the sound of the two Harleys driving away from Monmouth.

She pulled out the mixing bowls from the cabinets and slammed them on the counter.

"What's all this noise?" Mrs. Spell came rushing through the kitchen door. She gave Lilliana a horrified look. "It sounded like the whole kitchen was coming down."

"Sorry, Mrs. Spell." Lilliana sighed. "I'm just frustrated."

Mrs. Spell gave her a knowing look. "And would you be frustrated over Killian?"

"What?" Her eyes widened.

"Honey, I've been living long enough to know when a woman fancies a man." She grinned and walked over to the cabinet. She pulled down two crystal wine glasses and the bottle of red wine she kept for the dinner guests. She set them on the counter and proceeded to pour wine into both glasses.

She handed one to Lillian.

"Thank you." Lilliana took a sip and looked at the woman over the rim of her glass. "Is it that obvious?"

"Yes. And I think he likes you too." Mrs. Spell took a sip.

"Really?" She tried to play it cool. "I mean, he's been very kind. I just wasn't sure of his feelings."

"Men don't ever voice their feelings, honey. That's why you have to speak to them through their stomachs." She smiled brightly. "The only thing men like as much as hoochie coochie is food."

Lilliana bit her lip to stifle a laugh.

"Now I'll just leave you to get started on your baking." Mrs. Spell took another dainty sip of her wine and headed out the door.

"Certainly wasn't expecting that to come out of her mouth," Lilliana muttered. She took another sip of wine and then began gathering her ingredients to start baking Hummingbird Cakes.

CHAPTER 37

Killian and Brutus had been driving for almost five hours. He loved riding his Harley at night. Something about the darkness and the cool air always made him feel more alert and alive.

He was grateful that the forecasted rain had held off. He didn't really mind driving in the rain, but he didn't trust other drivers.

He glanced at the time on the Harley's dash. By now, Lilliana would be finished baking her cakes, and she'd soon be taking them over to the Natchez Bakery after she got some sleep.

He really didn't want her involved with this whole thing, but right now she had to keep up appearances. She had to keep doing it until he could track down whoever was responsible for distributing the drugs.

He checked his tracker on his phone. The truck had turned off the next exit in Memphis.

He eased into the right lane and took the exit. Brutus followed.

There was still activity in the city of Memphis, even in the early morning hours. He inhaled the scent of asphalt and gasoline.

It was a lot different than the sleepy town of Natchez.

He shook his head and glanced at the tracer map on his dashboard. He was quickly closing in on where the delivery trucks had been headed.

He finally slowed his speed as he came upon the industrial part of town. He drove a few more blocks until he came to his destination.

The Silver Moon Strip Club.

Despite the late hour, there were a lot of cars in the parking lot. He found a place to park and killed his engine. Brutus parked beside him.

"It makes sense. A strip club is the best place to move drugs," Brutus said.

"Yep, plus all that cash flow can easily be laundered." Killian got off his bike and stood.

He looked around at his surroundings. The parking lot was surrounded with cyclone fencing with barbed wire at the top. "I hate leaving my bike here."

"I dare someone to touch my Harley. It will be the last thing they ever do before I put them in the ground." Brutus growled.

"Let's do this." Killian started for the door with Brutus at his side.

The bouncer outside the door barely gave them a glance before opening the door for them.

They stepped inside, immediately hit with the scent of cigarette smoke.

"I fucking hate humans," Brutus groused. "Why the hell would you willingly inhale smoke?"

"No idea. Just try to blend in," Killian muttered.

"Yeah. Right." Brutus snorted and headed toward the bar.

Killian ordered a beer from a passing waitress. She smiled and leaned in too close before she headed off to fill his order.

He eased into a seat at a small table and assessed his surroundings.

The place was lit with blue and pink lighting. The stages where the strippers danced were illuminated with spotlights. There were only a couple of dancers on the smaller stages and the place was crowded.

"Here you go, sweetie." The waitress set the beer on the table.

Thanks." He gave her a ten-dollar bill.

Brutus slid into the seat next to him. He took a long pull on his beer.

"Ask for some dessert. That's what the bartender told me to say if I wanted something more than just a dance," Brutus stated.

"What if they think I'm talking about sex?" Killian gave him a grim look.

"Since when do you turn down sex?" Brutus arched his brow.

"Maybe I don't want meaningless sex with a stranger," Killian countered.

"Maybe you are stuck on a pretty human back in Natchez." Brutus smirked.

"Brutus, can I ask you something?"

"You will anyway."

"Have you ever thought about mating?"

"No." Brutus scowled. "I'm an Assassin. And we don't mate. Ever."

"And why not? I mean Guardians mate all the time."

"Yeah. And look at how that's all worked out," Brutus groused.

"Looks like it's working out just fine. Damon and Ava are happy and are having a baby. Lucien mated with Catty, and they are doing well. Hell, even Barrett mated with Jacey. And together they took down Boudier." Killian smirked.

"Yeah, but there's fallout from all that."

"Fallout. What are you talking about?"

"As males, we don't see it. How do you think Ava and Catty and even Jacey feel every time their mates leave out the door? Do you think they don't worry every second of the day when they are on a mission? Even though Barrett is Pack Master, he still has enemies. Especially with his position. He has a loyal following, but there's always someone out there wanting to take what is his."

"But we are Assassins. We are different than Guardians."

"We move in the shadows and exact justice on those who deserve it. Our position is more dangerous than a Guardian."

Killian sighed. "You really aren't a romantic at heart, are you, Brutus?"

"I am a realist and a survivor. That's why I know how to live off the land and make possum sausage."

"And why you never get laid." Killian snorted.

"Dude. I assure you, I get more ass than you ever did."

Killian stared at the Were. "As long as I've known you, I have never seen you pick up a female at a bar."

"I don't pick up females at bars. I have other ways."

"Like paying for it?" Killian gave him a strange look. "Dude, that can be dangerous. I mean you don't know if she's going to steal from you or what her background is or—"

"Relax. Asshole. I don't pay for sex. Don't have to." Brutus graced him with a smirk.

"Brutus, you never fail to surprise me." Killian shook his head and took another drink of his beer.

"Hey, baby. I'm Mercedes." A petite blonde sauntered up to their table wearing nothing but a bikini top and some incredibly short shorts. "Can I interest you in a personal table dance? We can go over to one of the rooms for some privacy." She smiled.

She was beautiful and had a great body. But she had too much makeup on and smelled like cheap perfume and cigarette smoke. He preferred a particular brunette with beautiful eyes and a stubborn streak.

"I'm not interest…"

Brutus cleared his throat and kicked him under the table.

Killian scowled and looked at Brutus.

"I think he's looking for something else. Something sweeter," Brutus stated.

Killian blinked. Understanding washed over him. He looked back at the waitress. "I actually was looking for some…dessert."

He felt like a complete idiot even asking. But if this is how you got drugs then he was going to look like an idiot.

"Ah." Her smiled spread across her face. "I see. And I think we have exactly what you want." She reached for his hand and pulled him to his feet. "And after you have a taste of this dessert, you may want a little something extra." She winked and licked her lips.

He resisted the urge to pull away.

He knew then that Lilliana had his heart. And she always would.

He followed Mercedes toward one of the private rooms. All the rooms had glass doors. He passed a few, and each one had a guy getting a lap dance with a topless dancer. They were not supposed to touch the dancers, but he guessed if you were in a private room, all rules were off the table because there was a lot of touching going on.

"Here we are." She led him inside and shoved him down on the couch. She went to the wall and pressed some buttons. Slow music spilled into the room.

Unease snaked up his spine. He sat up ready to exit the room if Mercedes started taking off her top.

"Relax, baby. In order to get the 'dessert,' you have to get an appetizer first." She nodded toward the bar. "They need to make sure you're not an undercover cop." She blinked and frowned. "You're not a cop, are you?"

"Fuck no. I'm no cop." Killian growled.

"Good. Then settle back and I'll give you what you need."

CHAPTER 38

Lilliana frowned and read and then reread the text on her phone.

Emmett Reece had sent her a text early in the morning insisting she deliver the cakes at five instead of seven.

She punched in his number and didn't have to wait long before he answered.

"Lilliana, I see that you got my text. About time. I've been waiting to hear back for half an hour."

"And good morning to you too," she said dryly. She sat up in bed and turned on the bedside lamp. "I worked late into the night and fell asleep. Sorry I'm just now returning your text."

"I need those cakes now. I hope you have them ready for me."

"Yes. I just finished about an hour ago. I was hoping to get some sleep before bringing them over," She groused.

"There's no time for that. I need those cakes now." Emmett's impatient tone had her on edge.

"Is there a problem?" She tried her best to keep the anxiety out of her voice.

"Yes, there is."

Her gut clenched.

"The buyer of these cakes is coming by at five thirty this morning to pick them up. If they're not here then you don't get paid."

And you don't get your drugs delivered, she thought to herself.

"That's an odd time to be picking up cakes," she ventured.

"It's for a large company meeting in Jackson. He's going to transport them himself."

"Let me throw on some clothes and I'll bring them over."

"There's no time for that. I'm sending a truck over to pick them up. I told them to pull up around the back of Monmouth. Just be at the back door so they can get the cakes and load them."

She sighed. "Fine. I'm walking over there now." She hung up the phone and quickly tugged her jeans, sweater, and boots on that she'd worn the other night. She'd take a shower before she got ready to cook for the guests.

After that, she was going to sleep the day away. Until Killian got back.

And then they'd talk.

She hurried down the small path to the back of Monmouth. All the lights were out in the mansion. Not even Mrs. Spell was up this early.

That was good. She didn't really want the woman to see the delivery truck for her cakes. She knew what the old woman would say. She'd say it was one thing for Lilliana to quietly sell her cakes for some extra cash, but it was quite another to have a truck pulling up to the back of the house for pickup. She would say it would mess up Monmouth's reputation and ambiance.

She rubbed her eyes and dug the key out of her jeans pocket.

She opened the door just as the rumble of a truck pulled up behind her. She gave a quick wave and then stepped inside the kitchen. She left the back door open and turned on the lights. She looked at her cakes all lined up on every available space in the kitchen. They were sitting on the kitchen counter, stove, island, and even the kitchen table. She'd already boxed them up in the white cake boxes.

She hated looking at them like that. She knew what they were being used for, and she felt guilt consume her.

"You Lilliana?" a deep voice said behind her.

A chill ran up her spine, and she turned. "Yes."

She froze.

"Hey, I know you." The human with hard familiar eyes glared at her.

She recognized him too.

"I don't think so." Her words squeaked out.

"Yeah, I do." He took a step closer and grabbed her arm. "You're the girl from the warehouse. The one I shot." He glared. "I'm either a bad shot or you're a werewolf."

"She's not a wolf. She's too scared to be a wolf." Emmett Reece stepped inside the kitchen.

She jerked her head over to Emmett. Her eyes grew wide. "What? Are you crazy?"

Emmett snorted. "Don't think I don't know about that? I guess you are going to deny it to protect that long-haired boyfriend of yours. Wouldn't want his secret of being a werewolf to get out, would we?" A slow sinister smiled stretched across his lips.

She felt the blood drain from her face to her stomach in a nauseating rush.

She shook her head. "You're on drugs."

Emmett snorted. "You didn't know did you?" He let out a laugh. "To have an animal in your bed and not even know it. You must be dumber than I gave you credit for."

"It's impossible." The words slipped through her lips.

"What is? That werewolves exist? Or that you didn't know you were fucking one?"

His cruel words cut her to her core. She looked up at him.

"I know a lot more than you think, Lilliana." Emmett glared at her. "I am disappointed that you got mixed up with all this. I was hoping to keep you under control and busy making your little cakes while I made the big money."

She tried to jerk free from the large man. He tightened his hold, pulled out a gun, and aimed it at her head.

"I wouldn't if I were you. Not this time. This time I promise I won't miss." He snarled.

"How could you, Emmett? You had a good life with a respectable bakery. But selling drugs?" She swallowed back the fear and lifted her chin in a sign of bravado.

He shook his head like she was a simpleton.

"I have a business that does okay. Do you know how much time and energy I've sunk into that bakery? Business was supposed to pick up, and I was supposed to be growing my income every year. But I can't do that in this economy. I look around at all the other restaurants and businesses doing well and growing. And it fucking pisses me off. They don't deserve the success and money they've gotten." He shoved his glasses up on his rather large nose and glared. "So when I was approached by someone who wanted to use my bakery as a way to make and move drugs, I jumped on it. I am making ten times what I was making before. All I have to do is let their hired men make the drugs at my place while I put them in Ziploc bags and stick them in the middle of cakes. It's brilliant actually. If the delivery truck ever gets stopped by the cops and searched, all they will see is the cakes."

Nausea rolled in her stomach. "I can't believe I was part of this."

"Yes, and no one would have believed that you weren't a

willing participant if you had just kept your nose out of my business and focused on staying in the kitchen."

She glared. "You had such a wonderful business. You've ruined it."

"No, I haven't. But you tried. You and that werewolf on that motorcycle"

Her eyes widened. "Why do you think he's with me?"

He smiled. "When you two broke into the warehouse and you got shot, I wanted a description of the couple. The girl sounded a lot like you, and well, they described the male as looking like a biker rock star. I remember seeing him at the bakery. I sold him one of your cakes by accident."

Her blood ran cold, and she wrapped her arms around her chest. "The house is full of guests, I'm sure you wouldn't want me to scream and alert them to what's going on in here."

"If you do, I'll just have him kill everyone in the house. It would be easy enough." Emmett shrugged. "That would make an interesting headline. Even kill old Mrs. Spell."

"Fine. Just kill me." Impending doom rushed through her. She was looking at her last day on earth.

Her mind flashed to Killian.

She would never see him again. Never hold him again. Never kiss him again.

"Kill you? Why would we kill you?" Emmett snorted. "I need you to keep making cakes so I can move my merchandise. But I can't leave you here either. So you are just going to have to come with me." He sneered.

"What about Mrs. Spell? She'll call the cops if I don't show up to cook breakfast today." Her heart galloped in her chest.

"Not unless you leave her a note telling her you quit."

"But I ..."

"But what?" Emmett stepped forward and got into her

face. "You don't have a choice, Lilliana. You can either refuse to go, and I'll kill you and everyone in this house. Or you can tell Mrs. Spell you quit, and come with me before anyone else gets hurt."

She knew in her gut he wasn't lying. He would have no reservations about taking a life no matter who it was.

"I'll go with you," she said quietly. She clasped her trembling hands in front of her. "I need to go wake up Mrs. Spell and tell her I'm quitting."

"There's no time for that." Emmett walked over to the refrigerator and grabbed the magnetic notepad off the door. He pulled open drawers until he found a pen.

"Here." He shoved them at her. "Make it quick." He looked at the guy pointing the gun at her. "Make sure she doesn't write a help me note. I'll start loading the cakes."

Blinking back the sharp tears, Lilliana pressed the pen to the paper and quickly scratched out her resignation.

Killian cringed as Mercedes took off her top and shoved her breasts in his face.

He really wasn't into her, and she had to know it by his body language. But he was on a mission and didn't want to blow his cover.

"Mercedes, you're getting a little too close to the clients." A large man wearing a black T-shirt stood in the doorway. He glared at Killian as he addressed the topless stripper. Killian held his gaze.

"He asked for dessert." Mercedes turned and started grinding her ass against Killian's crotch.

"Coming up." The man shot Killian one more look and then disappeared.

A few seconds later, another stripper with long, black hair and dark eyes appeared. She was wearing a bright-blue outfit that barely covered her breasts and ass. She was also carrying a tray with a slice of apple pie.

"Here ya go, baby. The best dessert money can buy."

She set the tray down on the table. He noticed a small

plastic bag of what appeared to be drugs poking out underneath the dessert plate.

"That will be ninety." Mercedes slid off his lap and turned around to face him.

He looked at both strippers and reached for his wallet. He pulled out a hundred-dollar bill. "Keep the change." He stood, swiped the drugs out, and stuck them in his pocket.

He stepped out of the room and looked around for Brutus.

He found the Were at the bar. He was trying to ignore two eager strippers wanting to give him a private lap dance.

He shook his head and walked over.

"Excuse us, ladies, but my friend and I need to be leaving." He slapped Brutus on the shoulder.

"But we were just getting to know him." The red-haired stripper pouted.

"Yeah. We hardly ever get cute guys like you two in here." The blonde purred and rubbed her hand down Killian's chest.

He grabbed her hand and gave her a smile. "Sorry. Duty calls, ladies."

"Oh, cool. Are you two in the military?" The redheaded woman's eyes widened in appreciation.

Killian grimaced and looked at Brutus. The Were was as stoic as ever.

"We love a man in uniform." The other stripper sighed.

"Yeah, well, we're both already taken. Sorry, ladies." Killian nodded at Brutus, and they both made their way over to the front door.

"Did you get it?" Brutus asked.

"Yeah. And now we know where they are distributing the drugs. Once we get back to Natchez, we'll go back to the bakery and find out where the base of operations is. It has to be somewhere inside that building. We have to take it down from there to put it out for good."

"And you're sure Lilliana isn't part of this?" Brutus asked as he stepped out the door. The early morning air was sharp and refreshing. It was a welcome change from the smoke-filled building they had just been in.

"I'm sure." He slid onto his Harley Davison Breakout and pulled his phone out of his pocket. "Let me check in with her before we leave."

"Dude, you're so pussy-whipped." Brutus snorted and saddled his bike.

"Am not." Killian growled and punched in her cell number.

He glanced at the time on his watch. It was early, but she was used to getting up so she could make her delivery before cooking breakfast for the guests at the house.

He frowned and hung up.

"What's wrong?" Brutus grunted.

"She's not answering."

"She's busy. Or maybe she doesn't want to talk to you."

He shook his head. "No, that's not it." He looked his friend in the eye. "Brutus, I have a very bad feeling."

"Fuck. I hate your gut instincts." He grimaced.

"But they are never wrong." Killian stuffed the phone back in his pocket and started the engine.

They had to get back to Natchez fast.

CHAPTER 40

Lilliana stood in the back of the Natchez Bakery and glanced over at Emmett. He, along with the hired goon who'd shot her, had taken her back to the Natchez Bakery after they loaded all the cakes in the back of the van.

She couldn't stop shaking. She'd never been this scared in all her life. She thought about Mrs. Spell. She felt bad about leaving Mrs. Spell a note without talking to her but it was better this way. She didn't want the older woman getting hurt.

If she ever got out of this mess, she'd have to start all over somewhere else. Right now that didn't scare her as much as the thought of dying.

"So what do you want from me? I already made the cakes for today." She looked over at Emmett and clasped her hands together to try to keep them from trembling.

"Since you won't be going back to Monmouth, you have more time to bake cakes. Instead of twenty cakes a day, I think we can double that amount." He sneered.

"I can't make that many cakes in a day." Her eyes went wide.

"Of course, you can. And you will. You see we know everything there is to know about you, Lilliana. We know that you have a mom who is still working, and she lives alone. Do you know how many dangers there are for women who are her age and live alone? Why, I can think of about twenty different ways that she might meet her death." Evil shone through his eyes.

Terror shot through her veins.

She swallowed back her fear. "Tell me what you want me to do. Just don't hurt my mother."

"Start baking."

"Fine" She walked over to the refrigerator and pulled out some butter.

"Not here. You'll cook in the basement." He pulled a key out of his pocket and held it out.

"I didn't know this place had a basement."

"I discovered it a few years ago. When I expanded my business, I made certain upgrades, shall we say." He walked over to one of the cabinets and moved some large canisters around. He stuck the key in a small opening in the back.

Suddenly, the wood floor opened up revealing a set of stairs.

"Ladies first." He smiled and waved her down.

She carefully made her way down the stairs into the darkness with Emmett following close behind. When she reached the bottom, Emmett flipped a switch on the wall, and the entire secret room lit up.

The area was big with an industrial-size kitchen. Pots and pans and mixers sat on the twenty-foot stainless-steel countertop. The floor was concrete, and the walls were cinderblock. Iridescent lights hung above on pendulous fixtures.

"It's not as nice as the kitchen up there." Emmett pointed to the ceiling. "But we're not asking you to make cakes that taste good. We are asking you to make cakes that will hold their shape so we can transport the drugs." He walked over to the far end of the darkened space. He flipped another switch.

The rest of the large room was bathed in lights. Another room, enclosed by a glass wall, had twelve people inside. All of them had large masks over their faces and were busy mixing up something like they were working in a lab.

None of them looked like they had had a bath in a month. One looked up and met Lilliana's eyes. He pulled down his mask and grinned, revealing a set of yellowed teeth.

Emmett walked over to her and handed her a mask. "Put it on."

She said nothing and complied. Once Emmett had his mask securely on his face, he walked over to the glass door of the wall and pressed some buttons.

The door swung open, and they both walked inside.

Despite the mask, Lilliana could still smell the rank odor of the drugs they were cooking. Crystal Meth.

"You will be working alongside these gentlemen here. They're not the same species as you and I. They are all wolves." Emmett's voice dripped with contempt. "You will bake the cakes, and once they have the drugs ready, you will put them in the middle of the cake and then frost them."

Nausea rolled over her in a rush.

"I don't think I can keep up with it. It takes a long time to bake a Hummingbird Cake and…"

"Then cut out the stuff you don't need in it."

"What?" She looked over at him and frowned.

"I don't need a Hummingbird Cake. I need something that resembles a Hummingbird Cake, so if that means you slap together a cake from a box then you do that. And leave out the bananas and pineapple."

She cut her eyes at him.

"Make it look nice. I don't care what it tastes like." He

snorted and headed out of the glassed-in room. She quickly followed.

The door locked behind them, but the workers were still staring at her. Could it be possible that what Emmett had said was true? Were they wolves?

"I don't think I can work down here with them." She lowered her voice.

"Why not?"

"Because if they are werewolves as you say, then it's too dangerous. What if they break out of that glass room and come for me?" She looked up at Emmett.

"They can't get out of that glass room. As long as you are doing your work and baking, they won't even bother glancing your way." He sneered.

She shook her head. Alarms were going off in her head. "You don't understand. I don't…."

"Shut your mouth!" He yelled. "If you say one more word, I will cut your tongue out."

She took a step back, shocked at his venom.

"Remember, you are not like your biker wolf. You are human. And a bullet to the head is fatal to you." He brushed an invisible piece of lint off his shirt. "Although I don't want to kill you. It would be a waste. I'll just maim you, just enough to keep you in line. Like cutting out your tongue. Then you won't be so mouthy."

She slammed her mouth shut.

Her blood ran cold in horror.

He threw his head back and laughed. "See, Lilliana, I knew you were a smart girl. Now I will leave you alone so you can start your work. And once I close this secret door, no one will hear what goes on down here. So don't even think about screaming. All you'll do is get those boys in that glass room all riled up. And we don't want that, do we?"

"No." She broke out in a cold sweat across her body. Even

if Killian did come looking for her, he would never know she was down here.

She watched Emmett climb the stairs. When he shut the secret door behind her, she felt confusion and terror well up inside her.

She was alone. With no hope of ever leaving.

CHAPTER 41

Killian raced through the town of Natchez, not caring if a cop was going to pull him over or not.

Ever since he left Memphis, he'd been flying down the highway like the devil himself was after him.

Lilliana.

He had to get to her.

He hadn't realized it when he left, but as he drove his thoughts slid into place like a pieces in a puzzle.

She was pregnant. With his child.

He's smelled the change in her scent earlier. He hadn't even thought about pregnancy because it was unheard of for a human to bear and give birth to a werewolf's child. The sperm wouldn't fertilize the egg. Pregnancy for werewolves took a while. But he'd recognized Lilliana's scent because he'd smelled the same scent on Jacey, Barrett's pregnant mate.

The odds were not in their favor, yet she'd become pregnant with his child.

This was a game changer. Now he had to tell her exactly who and what he was.

And hope she'd still have him in her life.

He wanted a life with her and the child. He wanted her for life.

When he finally pulled into the driveway of Monmouth, he felt the tension in his shoulders loosen. He parked in the back where the kitchen was. He needed to see her, to make sure she was okay.

"You're lucky you didn't get pulled over, Killian." Brutus pulled up beside him and killed the engine. "Driving like that is not how you keep a low profile."

"Not now, Brutus." He hurried up the steps to the back door. He opened the door and stepped into the kitchen.

He froze when he didn't see Lilliana. He glanced at his watch.

"Killian, we missed you at breakfast." Mrs. Spell stepped into the room holding a cup of tea.

Breakfast. That meant she was here and safe.

He blew out a breath. He had to find her and tell her who he was. And that he wanted to be with her forever.

"Sorry I missed breakfast. I bet it was wonderful." He gave the older woman an easy smile.

"You would be wrong. It was awful." She narrowed her eyes.

"It was?"

"Yes. It was. Because Lilliana up and quit on me." She slammed her tea cup down on the counter.

"What?" Dread swelled in his gut.

"I woke up to nothing more than a written notice scribbled on a notepad." Mrs. Spell shook her head. "She didn't even have the decency to use stationary. That girl. She certainly has let me down."

He grabbed the older woman by the arms and looked down at her. "Are you saying Lilliana isn't here?"

She shrugged out of his hold and gave him an odd look.

"That's what I'm saying. She quit. Leaving me high and dry with no breakfast for the guests." She pressed her gray hair into place. "Why, I had to bake some biscuits out of a can and scramble eggs again." She shook her head. "The guests are starting to complain."

Brutus walked into the room and stopped. "What's going on?"

"Lilliana isn't here."

"Think she ran?" Brutus cocked his head.

Killian leveled his gaze at the Were. "No. I think she was kidnapped."

Mrs. Spell gasped and pressed a hand to her chest. "Kidnapped? Whatever for? Besides, if she were taken, wouldn't her kidnappers ask for a ransom? Besides, she left a note saying she was quitting."

Ignoring the woman, Killian looked around on the counter. "Where's the note she left?"

"Right here." Mrs. Spell opened a drawer and pulled out a slip of paper.

He quickly read the contents and then handed it back to her. "Where's the pad she used."

Mrs. Spell frowned and walked over to the refrigerator. She pulled the notepad off and handed it to him. "Why do you want that? It's blank."

"Do you have a pencil?"

"Yes." She rummaged in a drawer and pulled out a pencil. He took it and lightly rubbed the side of the pencil lead against the paper.

The letters NB came out.

He held it up.

Mrs. Spell frowned. "NB? What's that? Some kind of ingredient?"

"No, it's a clue." He looked at Brutus. "I think I know where she's at."

"Let's go," Brutus murmured.

They headed for the back door. Mrs. Spell grabbed his arm.

He turned and faced the woman.

"Do you really think something has happened to Lilliana?" Worry creased her face.

"I think when this is over, you will need to give Lilliana an apology and a big raise." He headed out the door for his bike.

Lilliana managed to bake seven cakes in two hours. With the large industrial ovens and numerous cake pans, getting the batter mixed and poured wasn't that big of a deal. It helped that she didn't have to add the fruit and other secret ingredients that made her cakes so special.

She set the cakes on the cooling racks and turned her attention to mixing up the icing. She opened the cabinets only to find containers upon containers of store-bought frosting.

"Not only am I aiding criminals and their activity, but now I'm forced to used store-bought icing," She muttered to herself.

A tapping on the glass made her jump. She spun around and looked over at the group of men cooking crystal meth.

Three of them had stopped their work and had walked over to the glass to look at her.

Chills ran up her spine. She looked away. Something about them seemed inhuman.

Was Emmett telling the truth?

She glanced back. One of the men had pressed his face up

to the glass and was licking it while glaring at her with a mixture of lust and hatred. His dark eyes started to change. Suddenly they were yellow.

Fear squeezed her heart. She stifled a scream. What was going on? That wasn't humanly possible.

She forced her gaze back to the counter. She had a lot of layers to attach with frosting. She would just focus on her work and block the terror and fear out of her mind.

CHAPTER 43

Killian parked off the street near the Natchez Bakery. He killed the engine and slid off the bike. He waited impatiently for Brutus to do the same.

"What's the plan?" Brutus cracked his knuckles and looked around. Despite it being almost noon, there were very few people walking down the street. Even fewer parked in front of the bakery.

"The plan is to bust in there and get Lilliana out. Then I kill them all." He would protect her and their unborn child.

"So, you're saying you have no plan," Brutus said calmly. "You forget Killian, you have to think like a Guardian. And not an Assassin. You need a plan."

Killian jerked his head in the Were's direction. "Killing is what I do. It's who I am."

"Right. But you're also more than just a killer."

Killian froze. He wasn't sure what to make of Brutus's words. He opened his mouth to speak, but Brutus held up a gloved hand.

"Since I'm the smart one out of the group, I'll come up with the plan." He looked back at the bakery. "They know what you look like, but not me. I'll go in the front. I'll ask for a Hummingbird Cake and keep them busy. That should give you time to go in through the back door. If she's here, she won't be out in the open. I'm willing to bet that they are cooking the drugs right in the bakery."

"If they were doing that, then everyone could smell it. I mean crystal meth smells horrible."

"Not unless it was in a different part of the building." Brutus shook his head.

"I've been in there at night. I searched the whole building. I didn't find anything…" He met Brutus's gaze.

"What?"

"I didn't find anything except a key that didn't fit any of the doors."

"Then it fits a lock you haven't found yet." Brutus's eyes narrowed.

Killian looked back at the building. His gaze drifted to the storm drain in the front of the building. "What if they are cooking it underground. They could vent the smell through the sewage system. I bet humans couldn't even pick up on the smell."

"But we can." Brutus nodded. "Wait here and let me check it out before you go around back." He jogged over toward the bakery. He stopped when he reached the storm drain and pretended to tie his motorcycle boot. He glanced over his shoulder at Killian and gave a single nod. He had smelled meth.

Relief flooded through Killian. Now he knew where the drugs were being made and that Lilliana was being held underground.

Now all he had to do was find her.

CHAPTER 44

Brutus stepped inside the Natchez Bakery and stopped. The place was nearly empty except for one little old lady who was waiting impatiently at the counter.

There was no one waiting on her.

He stepped up beside her.

She turned and narrowed her yes. "Now listen here, young man. Don't you think about cutting in line."

"I wouldn't think of it." Brutus grunted.

"You say that, but when someone comes out here, they will go straight to you and completely ignore me." She pointed her finger at him.

"I know how to wait my turn," he assured her.

"I'm sick and tired of coming in here and not getting what I want."

He turned and looked down into her old eyes and wrinkled face. "So why do you keep coming here?"

She pressed her lips into a thin line. "Because I keep hearing how they are selling out of those Hummingbird Cakes. And by golly, I'm getting me one today. I'm not getting any younger you know."

"You don't want one of those cakes." He faced the counter.

"Why not?"

"Because they aren't worth the money. A Twinkie Cake is way better." He leaned over the counter and caught the eye of a tall, thin man in the back. The man nodded and held up a finger before finishing a conversation with someone in the back.

"Lady, I think you might want to leave." He felt for the Sig Sauer in his holster. "There may be some trouble."

"There's going to be trouble alright. I'm going to sue this place for ageism."

"Age what?" He frowned and looked at her.

"Ageism. It's when they discriminate because they won't sell to me because of my age." She lifted her chin. "I raised eight children, been married multiple times, and have volunteered every week at church bingo. I deserve this cake." She slapped her hand on the counter. "I'm not leaving this bakery until I get a Hummingbird Cake."

"Fine. But it will probably kill you." He sighed and focused his attention on the tall man walking out of the back.

"Lots of things can kill me. I'm not afraid of raising my cholesterol level." She glared at him.

"Can I help you?" The tall man stepped behind the counter and looked from the old woman back to him.

Brutus looked in the back and saw a flash of black. He knew Killian had made it inside. All he had to do was keep the man occupied until Killian could get Lilliana out of the building.

"I want a Hummingbird Cake." He and the old woman spoke in unison.

Brutus looked at the woman and glared. She shot daggers with her eyes right back.

"I'm afraid we don't have that product today. You see another buyer bought all we had." The man looked at Brutus.

"You're lying," the old woman shouted. She pointed at the tall cake behind the glass case. "There's one right there."

"And that one is already sold as well." The old man stated. He looked back at Brutus. "But if the gentleman would like to place an order for tomorrow, I'm sure I can accommodate."

"Why you little dried up, sniveling, beak-nosed weasel," the woman shouted. "I'm in front of him. I'm next in line to place an order. Not him." She shoved her thumb in Brutus's direction.

"I'm sorry, ma'am. But he was here first." The man glared.

"You are a liar," Brutus stated.

"Excuse me." The man's lips thinned, and he leaned over the counter.

Brutus knew from the man's scent he was human. He also knew that the man should be intimidated by him, but he clearly wasn't.

"I said you are a liar. The old woman was here before me. She was waiting when I walked inside." He crossed his arms over his chest.

"Is that so?" He cocked his head. "Well, maybe I don't want to sell her a cake or you a cake for that matter."

"See." The old woman shoved her finger at the owner and looked at Brutus. "I told you he hates old women. That's against the law, you know." She glared.

"You know what else is against the law? Disturbing the peace. I'm calling the cops." He lifted his chin in the air.

"You do that, asshole. Go ahead. I'm sure the good police department of Natchez will be interested to know of your other business dealings. The illegal ones." Brutus sneered.

The man's eyes widened and then he glanced at the doorway he'd walked out of. He motioned with his head.

Three large, hired men armed with assault rifles walked out.

He stepped in front of the woman and narrowed his eyes. "Let the old lady go, and we will settle this."

"I'm not going anywhere until I get me a Hummingbird Cake."

Brutus sighed and looked over his shoulder. "Are you blind or just crazy? They have guns. Really, really big guns."

"Honey, do you think that makes me scared?" She dug around in her purse and pulled out a .44 Magnum. She waved it around with her finger on the trigger.

Everyone took a step back.

"Easy lady." The owner visibly paled. He looked to Brutus for help. "Can you get your grandma under control?"

"Grandma? Do I look like I'm his grandma?" She waved the gun in the air.

All three men plus the owner's gaze were trained on the old lady. One of the men slowly lifted the gun.

Brutus pulled his 9 mm and aimed it at the male. "Easy, buddy. You want to make sure you can walk out of this, right? No use going out in a body bag."

"I'm not afraid to die." The guy met his gaze, and a sadistic smile crossed his face. His teeth were yellowed from drug use, and his eyes were glazed.

Fuck. He knew the guy was high on meth.

And meth heads were unpredictable.

CHAPTER 45

Killian waited until Brutus headed inside the Natchez Bakery before he went around to the back of the building. He stopped short when he saw two large men guarding the back door.

He knew then that Lilliana was inside. Otherwise, why would they have men posted at the door?

They turned and glared as he approached.

"You're not allowed back here." The large guy with muscles and no neck stepped toward him.

"I was wondering if you could help me. I'm looking for a girl."

"Look, asshole. You need to leave. Before you get your ass handed to you." The second guy stepped up and curled his fingers into meaty fists.

"Now see. That right there is not very nice." Killian lost the smile and growled.

"I'll show you not nice." The guy reached his arm back and threw a punch. Killian dodged it and threw his body against the man. They landed on the ground with a loud thud.

He plowed his fist into the man's jaw and looked up just in time to see the second guy pull a gun out of the back of his jeans. He aimed it at Killian.

But Killian was faster. He leapt to his feet. The gun went off.

He tackled the second guy to the ground and grabbed a nearby brick and hit him in the face. The guy's eyes rolled back in his head, and a trickle of blood ran down out of his nose.

Killian got to his feet, his blood pumping furiously through his veins.

He didn't have much time left. Everybody inside the building would have heard the gunshot, and they would be rushing outside to see what the problem was.

He picked up the two guns, unloaded them, and threw them in the dumpster near the door.

He opened the back door and hurried inside to find Lilliana.

CHAPTER 46

Lilliana froze at the faint noise. It was barely audible. What-ever it was had to have been big for her to hear. She looked up at the ceiling.

"Killian," she whispered to herself. Was he here? Had he tracked her back to the bakery?

She looked over at the glass room. The men had stopped working and were all looking at her with unveiled lust in their eyes.

Danger hung heavy in the air.

If they got out of that room then all hell was going to break loose.

She needed to prepare.

One of the men grabbed a metal scale he'd been using to weigh the crystal meth. He held it high in the air and brought it down hard on the glass wall.

She jumped.

The glass held.

But she knew it wouldn't hold forever.

The other men realizing what he was doing, looked

around for something else to help break the glass encasement they were in.

Fear swelled inside her chest.

If they got out, she knew what they'd do to her. Horrible, unspeakable things. And when they were done, they'd kill her.

She swallowed back her fear and looked around the kitchen for something to use to defend herself. What if they really were werewolves, like Emmett said. What the hell could she use against them?

She tugged open drawers, rifling through the array of mixing spoons.

No knife could be found.

"Shit." She shoved her hair back away from her face. Of course. They wouldn't leave a weapon for her. She might use it on her captors.

The men banged on the glass harder. She jumped and looked around. A tiny crack in the glass had started to develop.

She didn't have much time.

She ran up the stairs and banged on the floor. She screamed, hoping for a miracle that she could be heard.

The sound of glass shattering on the concrete floor like icicles falling to their death washed over her.

Her time was officially up.

CHAPTER 47

Killian heard the sound. It sounded so far away, and he knew human ears couldn't even hear it.

But he did.

It was the scream of a female.

"Lilliana," he breathed out her name. He raced inside and into the kitchen. The room was empty, and he looked around frantically. He opened the pantry, looking for a secret door.

Nothing.

He lifted his head back and growled.

That's when he felt it. A tiny tremor against his foot.

He looked down at the floor.

He felt another tremor against his foot.

A gunshot rang out through the building. He jerked his head in the direction of the front of the store.

Brutus.

He heard the distinct growl of Brutus. Whoever was shooting at him was going to be in a world of hurt from the Assassin.

He crouched on the ground and pressed his ear to the floor. He could smell her.

Lilianna was here.

He looked around, trying to find a way to get to her.

"Fuck." He growled in frustration. He slammed his fist to the ground. The floor moved under his hit. He hit it again. If he had to dig out the whole fucking floor to get to her, then he'd do it.

The wood floor moved a little. That's when he saw it. A seam down the middle of the floor.

He stood and grabbed a knife off the counter. The sound of fighting and gunshots rang out in the background. He knew Brutus could handle himself. Right now, he had to get to Lilliana.

He stuck the blade into the seam of the wood and twisted. The floor slid back far enough that he could get his fingers inside.

"Killian!" Lilliana screamed as she pressed her face to the opening.

"I'm coming for you. Move back."

"Hurry. They are almost out. Killian, they are coming to get me."

"Who?" He frowned and stuck both hands in the opening.

"The men making meth. They have terrible yellow eyes. I don't think they are human." She trembled.

Anger and horror crawled around in his gut until he thought he was going to be sick.

Emmett must be working with red wolves. They were the only werewolves who made crystal meth and sold other drugs to make a buck.

If the red Weres got to Lilliana, they would rape her until they killed her.

Old instincts and habits rose up in his soul.

He gritted his teeth and pulled at the opening. Throwing back his head, he yelled as the floor slowly slid apart.

"Killian!" Lilliana screamed. Her face disappeared from

the opening as they pulled her away. The stench of red were-wolves floated up to his nostrils.

He cursed and pulled at the opening with all his strength. The floor slid apart, revealing a staircase leading underneath the Natchez Bakery.

Lilliana screamed again.

He raced down the stairs. When he got to the bottom, he found himself surrounded by ten red Weres, each one holding a metal object.

One red Were had Lilliana by the neck and was holding her in front of him like a shield.

"Easy, wolf. You don't want me to hurt this female, do you?" The red Were sneered and slid his dirty hand underneath Lilliana's shirt to grab her breast.

"Don't touch her." Killian reached in his jeans pocket for a hair tie. Rage clouded his vision, and the automatic actions of being an Assassin came back to him like an old habit.

He pulled his hair back and secured it in a knot, revealing the Assassin's tattoo to his enemy.

"Fuck." One of the reds dropped his weapon and took a step back. "I know who you are."

"You will all know who I am before I leave this room." His words were cool like white lightening. He always killed upon command. Now, for the first time, he wanted to kill because he wanted revenge.

"Who is he, Sam?" The one holding Lilliana laughed. "Santa Claus?"

"Fuck no. He's Killian. The Assassin." Sam grew pale and tried to make a run for the stairs.

Killian spun around and grabbed the red Were by the neck. He picked him up over his head and slammed him to the concrete floor. The Were cried out in pain and tried to move. Killian didn't give him a chance. He pulled his silver knife out of his boot and buried it into the base of his skull killing him instantly.

Blood spread across the concrete.

"You motherfucker." One of the Weres shifted into wolf form took a step toward Killian.

Killian met his glare and smiled. He threw his knife into the ceiling to keep the others from getting it. If they wanted to play with the wolf then they were going to get the wolf.

He tugged off his jeans. He didn't bother with his shirt. The other Weres knew where this was headed and looked at each other.

He called to the wolf inside and shifted. The pain and pleasure of shifting always excited him. As an Assassin he didn't get to kill much in his wolf form. Usually he killed in his human form. But this was personal and he was going to kill them all for hurting Lilianna.

The red wolf launched himself at Killian. Killian leapt and met him in the air. They fell to the ground with the red wolf on top. The wolf bit Killian's shoulder. Pain raced through his arm and chest.

He heard Lilianna scream.

He twisted his body and gained the advantage. He pinned the red wolf to the ground and sunk his teeth into his neck. Blood spurted and the red wolf howled it pain. Killian didn't care.

He bit harder and pulled. The red wolf's eyes grew wide realizing Killian's intent.

Killian ripped out his enemy's throat.

He looked around the room, blood dripping from his mouth.

The red Weres scattered, each trying to get out of the room. Each trying to get past Killian to freedom. He jumped into the air and grabbed the knife with his mouth.

He landed on his feet and shifted back to human form.

"You should not have touched her," Killian's voice was low and deadly. One by one, he grabbed the red Weres stuck the silver knife into each one's head. He slaughtered them all until there was only one left.

When he looked at the red Were holding Lilliana, Killian threw the knife.

The knife sunk into the red Were's forehead. The red wolf crumpled to the ground.

"Lilliana, are you alright?" Killian's gaze was glued on her.

Wide-eyed, she took a step back. "You lied to me. You're a werewolf. And a killer."

CHAPTER 48

Lilliana looked at the male she loved standing in front of her. He was covered in blood. And his eyes looked different to her. He looked like a lethal killing machine.

"You told me you were an investigator."

"Actually, you came to that conclusion on your own. My mistake was not correcting you." He rubbed his neck and looked away.

She curled her hands into fists. "Killian, you're a werewolf. You never said anything about being a werewolf. And you never said anything about killing people. They called you an Assassin." She swallowed back her fear and confusion.

"I'm an Assassin for werewolves. Once someone commits a crime against the Pack and if it's serious enough then I'm one of the three Assassins they send out to execute the sentence." He looked at her. Under the blood and anger shining in his eyes, she saw a semblance of the male she'd given her body to.

"The sentence of death." She looked away.

Brutus headed down the steps and stopped at the bottom. "What the fuck happened here?"

"Just taking care of business."

"You feel better now that you're back to being an Assassin?" Brutus arched his brow.

Killian looked at him. "Actually, yes. Thanks for asking."

"Put your fucking jeans back on. No one wants to look at your junk." Brutus looked over at her and cocked his head. "You okay?"

"I... I honestly don't know. I'm guessing you're a werewolf too?" No wonder he looked so dangerous to her.

Brutus narrowed his eyes and opened his mouth to answer.

"Big boy!! Hey, big boy, where did you go?" A familiar female voice called out from the top of the stairs.

Brutus cringed.

"Big boy? Brutus, who the hell is that?" Killian leaned over and peered up at the top of the stairs.

"That's Edith," Brutus muttered.

"Oh my God. Edith. Is she hurt?" Lilliana rushed over to the stairs and looked up.

Killian looked back at Brutus. "Who is Edith?"

"I'm big boy's backup," Edith called out from above.

Brutus blushed and shoved his hands in his jeans pocket.

"She pulled out a .44 when the owner wouldn't sell her a Hummingbird Cake. She was waving the gun around when it went off." Brutus cracked a smile. "Those guys shit themselves. That's when the shooting broke out. Two guys are dead. But the owner is alive and secured upstairs."

"And she didn't get hit?" Lilliana asked Brutus.

"Edith?" He snorted. "No. She may be old, but she's as fast as a cat. Plus, she's a were...."

"A werewolf?" Lilliana frowned and looked at the top of the stairs.

Edith smiled down at her. "Well, hello, honey. What are you doing down in that hole with that cutie pie, Brutus?"

"Cutie pie?" Killian arched his brow.

"Fuck off, Killian." Brutus glared.

Lilliana drug her gaze back up to Edith. "Edith, is it true. Are you a werewolf?"

"Sure is. You wouldn't know because you're a human and you couldn't smell me. But Brutus didn't know because I wear Chanel No. 5. I always heard it brought the men in." She gave Lilliana a wink. "Apparently it does more than that. It conceals my werewolf scent."

"Sounds like she'd be perfect for Lorcan." Killian shrugged.

"I suppose he's another Assassin?" She narrowed her eyes at the men in front of her.

Killian nodded.

Brutus looked between them and then addressed Killian. "I already put in a call to Barrett. He's busy at the moment so I left a message."

"What happens now?" Lilliana wrapped her arms around herself. "I mean, do we have to clean this up? Do I have to be interrogated?"

"I'm not cleaning this shit up. Assassins don't clean." Brutus started for the stairs.

She ventured a look at Killian. He turned his head, looking at all the carnage he'd caused. It was then she saw a tattoo on his neck.

"I don't think there's any way to clean this up. Besides, whoever Emmett is in business with will just start business back up. It's a perfect setup for a meth lab." Killian looked back at Lilliana.

"So what do we do?" Lilliana asked.

"I noticed this is the only building occupied on this block."

She nodded. "The other businesses all closed up years

ago. Nobody wants to open up a business in this part of town anymore." She frowned.

"Why do you ask?"

"Because I want to make sure there's nobody in the rest of the block." He looked at her. "I'm going to burn this fucker to the ground."

Her mouth dropped open. "How?"

He pointed to where the red Weres had been cooking the drugs. "They are venting to the sewer. Once a fire hits the methane gas, it will go up." Killian held out his hand. "But first I want you out of here."

She shivered and wrapped her arms around herself. "So the building will be destroyed."

"I'm sorry. It has to be. All the evidence about the drugs and werewolves has to be wiped out. The police will think it was a gas leak that led to the explosion and assume these bodies were a result of it."

She nodded. "I'll check the rest of the building for people. There may be some homeless or runaways that we may not be aware of.'

"I can do that." He swiped his face with the back of his hand.

"You'd better not. Anyone seeing you like that will call the police. And that's the last thing you need." She started up the stairs. "I would recommend at least washing the blood off your face and hands before you leave. And your chest, since you ripped your T-shirt to shreds when you…changed."

"It's called shifting."

"Shifting." She nodded and headed up the stairs, leaving the bloodied bodies behind her.

CHAPTER 49

Killian stepped out of the shower at Monmouth and wrapped a towel around his hips. It had taken him twenty minutes to get all the blood and tissue of the red werewolves out of his hair. By the time he was done, he was ready for a shot of whiskey and a long nap.

But he didn't have time for that. He had to get ready for Barrett's arrival. More importantly he had to talk to Lilliana.

After calling and updating the Pack Master on what had gone down, Killian had been ordered to stay where he was.

Barrett was on his way to see him, and he was bringing someone with him.

Killian towel-dried his hair and looked into the mirror. His gut sank every time he thought about the look on Lilliana's face after he'd executed the room of red Weres.

Killian had not mistaken Barrett's angry tone. Barrett knew about the executions and also that Lilliana had discovered the existence of werewolves.

Barrett pissed at him for rushing in and taking everyone down without a direct order.

He'd fucked things up bad this time, and he wasn't sure he could talk his way out of it.

A knock on the door made his heart jump in his throat.

Maybe it was Lilliana? He looked around for some jeans but remembered he was out of clean clothes. He had not anticipated getting all bloodied up on this trip so he hadn't packed very many jeans.

He tightened the towel around his hips and opened the door.

"Dude, that's the last thing I want to see." Lorcan cringed and covered his eyes. He shoved a pair of jeans and a T-shirt at him. "Here, for the love of God, put these on before I go blind."

"You wish you looked as good as me, Lorcan." Killian begrudgingly took the clothes. "You wanna come in?"

"Only if you promise to get dressed in the bathroom." Lorcan continued to shield his eyes.

"You're such a whiner." He opened the door and Lorcan stepped in. "When did you get here?" Killian stepped into the bathroom and quickly dressed.

"About an hour ago. I drove down to where the Natchez Bakery *used* to be before coming over here." Lorcan walked over to the window and gazed down. "You actually blew the whole block up."

Killian stepped out of the bathroom and cringed. "Yeah. I don't think Barrett is going to be happy."

Lorcan turned. "You think?"

Killian scrubbed his hand down his face. "I didn't have a whole lot of time to clean up the scene. Blowing up the building to make it look like a gas leak was the only option I had. And I guess I fucked up."

"I never thought I would hear you say that." Lorcan turned.

"Say what?" Killian sighed. "That I fucked up?"

"No. That you chose to blow up a building that makes… cakes." Lorcan grinned.

"You're such an asshole." Killian chuckled. For the moment, the weight of the world had shifted off his shoulders. He needed the relief.

"How is Lilliana?" Killian asked.

"Ah, yes. Lilliana. I was wondering how long it was going to take for you to ask about the human." Lorcan looked out the window. "She's beautiful, isn't she?"

Killian gritted his teeth. "Of course she's beautiful. You'd have to be blind not to notice." He sighed. "She's more than that, though. She's talented and smart and funny. And she has this annoying habit of being stubborn and not listening to anything I tell her."

Lorcan brightened. "Which makes me like her more."

Killian slumped into the chair by the window. "Lorcan, I …"

"You love her." Lorcan sighed. "I talked to Brutus."

"Brutus told you." Killian huffed.

"No, he didn't. But he did tell me about the carnage he saw in the basement of that bakery." Lorcan turned and faced him. "You are an Assassin, Killian. And you're good at what you do. Whenever we have had our assignments, you do your job without fail. And you do it nice and clean and without a lot of emotion." Lorcan cocked his head. "What Brutus said he saw in that basement was a lot of emotion. You killed them all because they threatened to hurt Lilliana. Only an emotion that strong would make you do what you did."

Killian buried his head in his hands. "It doesn't matter that I love her. She won't ever have me now. Now that I lied about what I was." He looked up. "Lorcan, you didn't see the way she looked at me after I killed them."

"She's never been around a werewolf before. Not to mention one that happens to be an Assassin. And I'm willing to bet she's never been around anyone, for that matter, who would kill for her." Lorcan shrugged.

"I don't think she'll look at me like before. She's scared of me, Lorcan."

"Then she needs to make a choice." Lorcan walked to the door. "To be with you or not." He shut the door behind him.

CHAPTER 50

"I'm so pleased to have you as our guests." Mrs. Spell handed him a glass of sherry. "Mr. Welbourn says you're from New Orleans."

"Thank you, Mrs. Spell. I appreciate your hospitality. And thank you for the room on such short notice. I'm actually from Arkansas. Just moved to New Orleans a few months ago." Barrett Middleton took a sip of the drink and tried not to grimace. He'd arrived in Natchez a few hours ago. He had called Jack Welbourn and informed him of what had happened. Jack was waiting for him at Monmouth Plantation with a few of his Mississippi Guardians.

Jack slapped him on the back a little too hard. "I invited him down here for a little visit and to do some business."

"Thank you so much, Jack, for choosing Monmouth." She smiled and patted her hair. If Barrett wasn't mistaken, the older woman blushed when she looked at Jack.

"Of course my dear." Jack grinned. "So is there a private room you can offer us for a quick meeting?"

"I'll show you to the library. No one will bother you in there, and please stay as long as you like. A lot of our guests checked out this morning." Mrs. Spell led them through the house to the library. She took a key out of the pocket of her sweater and unlocked the room. "With all that smoke from the fire of the Natchez Bakery, a lot of people didn't want to stay." She shook her head. "I told them it would be clearer in the morning and just to give it a day. But they wouldn't listen."

"Well, you'll have guests for tonight my dear. I hope you have a dinner planned?" Jack smiled.

Barrett wanted to roll his eyes. The Pack Master might be old, but he certainly still had it when it came to the ladies.

"Of course. And our cook is just amazing." Mrs. Spell frowned. "You know she up and quit on me this morning, but I guess she changed her mind. I was worried for a while, but she came back, and I agreed to give her a raise and more time off."

"How good of you, Mrs. Spell. I bet there is no one that can match your generous heart." Jack smiled warmly.

Barrett stepped inside the library and waited for Jack.

"I'll leave you two alone. Help yourselves to the bar. There's whiskey and bourbon and scotch. All top shelf." She closed the door behind her.

Jack turned and faced Barrett. His good mood was gone, and the smile slid off his face.

"Before you say a word, I want Killian in here. I want to get his side of the story," Barrett said slowly.

"Killian is an Assassin. Not a Guardian." Jack shook his head. "You should have sent someone else."

"I sent who I sent." Barrett walked over to the door and opened it. Two of the Mississippi Guardians were standing outside. They briefly nodded in submission to Barrett.

"Bring Killian to me."

"Absolutely." One stayed behind to guard the room while the other headed off on his mission.

Barrett closed the door and walked over to the bar. He set down the sherry.

"I don't see how you drink that shit," Barrett groused and reached for the bottle of bourbon. He poured two fingers in a glass and took a sip. He looked at Jack. "Now see, that's good."

"Give me that sherry. You don't waste alcohol. No matter what kind it is." He poured Barrett's sherry into his own glass.

There was a quick knock on the door.

"Enter," Barrett said and took a sip.

The door opened, and Killian stepped inside. His hair was still wet, and he was dressed in his usual color of black.

"You wanted to see me, Barrett." Killian stood in front of him with a resigned look on his face.

Barrett frowned. He wasn't used to seeing the happy-go-lucky Were look so serious.

"Killian, this is Jack Welbourn. As you know he's the Pack Master of Mississippi."

"Nice to meet you, Mr. Welbourn. I wish it were under better circumstances," Killian said politely.

"Why don't we all sit." Barrett walked over to the couch and took a seat. The other two followed.

"Killian, I have some questions for you." Barrett stared at him over his glass. "You were sent her for recon. And in less than a few days, you managed to involve a human in Were business. That human was shot and kidnapped. You also executed a roomful of werewolves in front of her in your wolf form. And to top it off, you burned down an entire block where the Natchez Bakery was located." He took a sip. "Is that correct or am I leaving anything out?"

CHAPTER 51

Killian grimaced and looked at his Pack Master. "It sounds way worse when you say it out loud."

"Why didn't you contact me when you found out they were shipping the drugs to that strip club in Memphis?" Barrett glared.

Killian took a deep breath and met his gaze. "Because I wanted to have Emmett Reece in custody and the situation contained."

"That's opposite of what happened," Jack muttered.

"You're right." Killian nodded. "When we got back to Monmouth, I realized Lilliana had been taken. She left a clue that she was at the Natchez Bakery. My goal was to get her out before apprehending Emmett Reece, who was manufacturing the drugs in the basement of the bakery. When I discovered that she was being held in a roomful of red Weres who were going to harm her…"

"You slaughtered them." Barrett finished the sentence.

"Wait, there were red Weres in the basement?" Jack straightened in his chair.

"Yes." Killian looked at him. "Emmett was using them to

cook the meth. They were cooking it in the basement and venting it out into the sewer."

"Humans would never know that's what was going on because they don't have our keen sense of smell," Barrett added.

"How many red Weres were there?" Jack set his glass down and waited for an answer.

"Twelve."

"Emmett knows about werewolves. I ran a background check, and he has never been in any kind of military so he wouldn't know about us from there." Barrett rubbed his temple.

"I can't believe there are red Weres in my state that were cooking meth." Jack frowned. "This won't look good. Not good at all." He shook his head.

"Well, nobody's going to know now. Not since Killian handled the problem." Barrett pointed at him with his bourbon glass.

Jack looked at him and cocked his head. "Tell me about the human."

"Lilliana Beckway. She works here at Monmouth. And she's a fabulous cook and baker. She had taken on some extra work by baking and delivering Hummingbird Cakes. Emmett Reece had the idea of taking the cakes and cutting out the middle. He would then load up the packages of crystal meth inside and that's how he would distribute the drugs to the Silver Moon Strip Club. I'm sure the Pack Master of Tennessee will be happy to get that information. Since we've burned up where Emmett was making the drugs, the supply chain is broken."

"Good thinking, Killian." Jack stood and held out his hand. Shocked, Killian took it.

"Does this mean you're not mad about me blowing up the Natchez Bakery?" Killian asked.

"I've already talked to the chief of police, and they are ruling it as a gas leak. He knows that any bones he might find in the building need to be dumped in the Mississippi River." Jack turned to Barrett.

"I have all I need. We have stopped one of the largest drug rings we have ever had in Mississippi. On top of that, we managed to kill some rogue red wolves. I need to go make some calls. I appreciate your help with this, Barrett."

Barrett stood and shook Jack's hand. "I'll see you for dinner."

Killian watched Jack leave the room and then looked over at Barrett.

"Well, if you don't need me, I need to find Lilliana."

"We are not finished, Killian. Sit," Barrett ordered.

Killian bit back a reply but obeyed.

CHAPTER 52

Lilliana watched as the older gentleman, Jack Welbourn, exited the room that Killian had been sequestered in. She'd not seen Killian since after the building blew up. Despite the lies he'd told her, she needed to go check on him to make sure he was okay.

She shook her head. That didn't even make any sense. Killian was a freaking werewolf. Of course he was okay.

She was the one that needed help. Mental help to be exact.

"They will be a while," Brutus said over her shoulder.

"Jeez." She jumped and spun around. "You could have given me a heart attack." She pressed her hand to her chest.

"Sorry. I forget that humans are so fragile." Brutus said stoically.

"I didn't mean a literal heart attack. Just a figure of speech." She glared and headed into the kitchen. He followed.

"I hear we are having a full table of guests tonight so if you don't mind, I need to start prepping." She lifted her chin.

"Killian likes you." Brutus cocked his head. "And that's unusual."

She turned and gave him her full attention. "That he likes someone?"

"No. That he likes you. You're not like the other girls he's been with."

"What do you mean?" Her heart jumped in her chest.

"He usually likes blondes with brown eyes." Brutus shrugged.

"Maybe he's changing it up." Her heart fell. He didn't like her; she was just another notch on his belt.

"No. He feels something for you that he's never felt before." Brutus sighed.

"Well, I guess it doesn't matter, does it? He lied to me about being a…"

"Say it with me. Werewolf."

"You know, you would think I would be a little more freaked out by this whole thing."

"You're not?" He frowned.

"I don't know. I mean, seeing him shift into a wolf was pretty crazy. I've always wondered about there being something more than what we see in everyday life. Plus I love the sci-fi channel." She shrugged and pulled out some vegetables and placed them on the cutting board. "Not that any of this matters. I'm pretty sure there are rules between humans and werewolves dating each other." She lifted her chin and pulled out a knife to chop the vegetables.

"Assassins don't mate. Not because they don't want to but because it's so unusual for them to find their one true mate." Brutus picked up a carrot and took a bite. He chewed thoughtfully. "I think it's fate's way of making sure we have a strong female who can handle what we do."

"Like seeing a room full of werewolves being slaughtering?" She shivered.

"Yeah. I've never seen Killian execute like that. He prefers a silver bullet to the head when he's doing his job. Instant death and it's clean. But when he saw that you were in danger, he went full-on possessive alpha." Brutus stared at her.

"He lied to you to keep you safe. He will always keep you safe. Now you have to figure out if you can handle that. Can you handle being loved by a Were like that?" He took another bite of the carrot and started for the door.

"Brutus, wait."

He turned. "Since I'm cooking dinner tonight, I was wondering what you think I should make for dessert. I'm pretty tired of Hummingbird Cake."

A ghost of a grin crossed his lips. He opened the door and tossed the next words out of his mouth. "Twinkie Cake. I think you should make Twinkie Cake."

CHAPTER 53

Killian waited for Barrett to speak. He was no pussy, but Barrett Middleton was putting him on edge.

"I know what you are going to say. And you're right." Killian looked at Barrett.

"What am I going to say?" He took a slow sip of his bourbon.

"That I fucked up. That I should have called and updated you about who was making the drugs and how they were being distributed. You are going to say I should have waited to go in the Natchez Bakery when I found out they took Lilliana."

"You are wrong." Barrett gave him a thoughtful look. "Well, you are partly wrong."

Killian waited to hear what the male was going to say.

"You should have updated me as soon as you knew where the drugs were being transported. But you did one thing right."

"Really? What's that?" Killian frowned. To him, he felt like he'd fucked up the whole entire operation.

"You did right by getting in there and getting the female out." Barrett nodded.

"Lilliana. Her name is Lilliana." She would probably never speak to him again. With her, he really fucked up.

"Lilliana." Barrett cocked his head. "If I were in the same situation, I would have let nothing stop me from getting to her and getting her to safety. I'm not really even upset about the mess you made with the red Weres. We did some digging, and they were part of Edward Boudier's original team who kidnapped Ava. For killing them, you get a pass." Barrett shrugged.

"And the building?"

"Not my state, not my problem." He nodded at the closed door. "It sounded like Jack wasn't so worried about it either."

"So I'm good to go?"

"Not so fast." Barrett set his glass down and stood. "I want you to be honest with me."

"Of course. I have nothing to hide."

"Are you happy with your life?"

"Of course. I love being an Assassin." He shrugged. "I didn't even mind doing the recon."

"Didn't find it too boring?" Barrett raised an eyebrow.

"It was actually a lot of work." Killian cringed. "Not as easy as I thought."

Barrett smirked. "No shit."

Killian studied the floor and then looked back at Barrett. "Barrett, I want to apologize. I went into this mission thinking it was beneath me. Once I got involved, I realized how much work Guardians really do and how much danger they face on a daily basis. I should have given you an update as soon as I found out everything. I apologize."

"Jesus. How bad did that hurt?" Barrett snorted and then took another drink.

"More than you will ever know." He sighed.

"Good." Barrett stood, drained the glass, and set it on the table. He walked over and slapped him on the back. "Glad that is all settled."

"That's it? You're not going to fire me? Kick me out of New Orleans? Strip my rank?" Killian eyed him warily.

"No. I think you still have bigger problems."

"Like what to do with Emmett Reece? I'm not sure we can hold a human in our prison system. He knows too much about Weres to just release."

Barrett grinned. "Emmett Reece is already handled. We went in to interrogate him about how he found out about the werewolves. Someone beat us to him."

"Who?" Killian frowned.

"A female Were by the name of Edith. Apparently she followed Brutus back to that warehouse on the outskirts of town. We had taken possession of the building and were holding Emmett there. Edith talked her way in and shot him."

"Damn. Did she say why?"

"Says he never would sell her a Hummingbird Cake." Barrett shrugged.

"Wow. I guess you never know."

"No, you don't." Barrett laughed. "I think you have someone else you want to talk to. A very pretty female who's in the kitchen." Barrett gave him a look.

"There's something else you need to know. You might want to get another drink."

"Fuck. What is it?" Barrett scowled.

"Lilliana is pregnant. With my child."

"How can that be? You were only here a few days."

"I know. I even wore a condom but it broke. I didn't really think anything about it at the time since I thought she couldn't get pregnant. But she is. And I want to be with her. If she will have me."

207

"You know that's against the rules." Barrett glared. "You need to realize that you can't have your cake and eat it too. It's either keep your job, or quit and be with the female."

Killian felt his world shift. "I respect you Barrett. But if being with Lilianna means I can't be an Assassin anymore, then I'm afraid I'm turning in my resignation."

Barrett's lips pressed into a thin line. "Fine. I need that in writing by tonight."

"You say your female knows how to bake?" Barrett cocked his head.

"She's an expert. Never had anything like it." Killian grinned.

"Good. Now you don't have the need for Jacey's cookies." Barrett glared.

Killian blinked. He had the feeling it was a warning. "Yes. Absolutely."

"Good. Now we're clear." Barrett eased back into the chair and picked up his drink.

Killian nodded and exited the room.

Now he had to face Lilliana. And try to convince her how much he needed her.

CHAPTER 54

She sensed him before he even walked into the kitchen. Her heart slammed into her chest. When he stepped into the room, longing washed over her.

She continued to chop the vegetables on the chopping board. She needed him to speak first.

"Hey." His deep voice washed over her like a warm wave.

She cleared her throat. "Are you done with your meeting with Barrett and Jack?"

"Yeah. I am." He stepped closer. Her resolve to not look at him waivered.

But she had to hold her own and listen to what he was going to say.

"Lilliana, I need to talk to you. And I would like to look you in the face when I do."

She put the knife down and took a deep breath. The last image she had of him was standing in that basement covered in blood.

She slowly turned.

He stood before her, dressed all in black. "I am sorry that

I lied to you. I wanted to keep you safe. I thought by not telling you I was a werewolf that I was keeping you safe. Instead, I put you in the path of danger." He swallowed. "Lilliana, I'm so sorry for that. I would never do anything to hurt you. I hope you know that."

"I've never seen anything like what you did in that basement," she admitted.

"I'm so sorry. I am not like that…normally. Well, not on a day to day basis." He grimaced.

She crossed her arms. "So when you have to go execute people, do you normally get that messy?"

"No. And I don't execute people. Only werewolves who've committed the vilest of crimes." He sighed. "I usually just shoot them in the head. With a silver bullet. Sometimes I stab them in the heart with my knife but never what I did in the basement." He forked his fingers through his hair. "It's just when I saw those red Weres trying to hurt you, all I wanted to do was kill every one of them." He studied the floor. "I know you probably think I'm some kind of monster."

Her heart broke for him. "You know, Brutus also said you don't normally kill like that."

"He's right. I don't."

"In fact, he said you did it because you loved me." She swallowed, waiting for his response.

He jerked his head up and looked at her with pleading in his eyes. "He said that?"

"Yes."

Silence stretched between them.

"Well, he's right." He took a step closer. "I do love you. I loved you the first time I saw you in the garden."

"And you spit out my cake?" She cocked her head.

"Yeah." He grinned and came closer until they were inches apart. "Lilliana, I know it's hard to see what I did and still want to be with me. But I love you. I want you to be my mate. Now and forever. I've already given my resignation to Barrett. I'm giving up being an Assassin so I can be with you."

Tears burned behind her eyes. "You did."

"Yes. I don't want to lose you." He bent his head and covered her lips in a kiss so full of love, she thought she would melt on the floor.

When he pulled away, he pressed his head to hers. "There's something else you need to know."

"What?" She looked up at him.

"Normally werewolves and humans don't mate and they certainly don't ever produce a child together." He pressed his hand to her stomach. "But despite the odds, you are pregnant."

"How in the world would you even know? We only had sex a few days ago."

"I can smell it on you." His eyes sparkled with love.

"But you wore a condom."

"It broke. You must have had those forever."

"I did. From high school." She blinked not really comprehending what he was telling her.

Pregnant. She was going to be a mother.

"I love you Lilliana. And I want to mate and marry you. I want to raise this child as a family." He held her hands between his. "Please say something, sweetheart."

"This is unbelievable."

"Most love stories are."

"I love you too, Killian."

He smiled. "Good, then it's settled. I need to go find a computer and type up a resignation for Barrett. To make it official." He pulled away, but she grabbed his hand.

"Wait. I don't want you to do that. Being an Assassin is part of who you are and why I love you. I would never ask you to choose between me and your brothers, Lorcan and Brutus."

"You wouldn't?" His eyes widened. "But Barrett already told me I had to choose. And I choose you."

"Let me go talk with Barrett." She took off her apron and set it on the counter. "I'll be right back."

CHAPTER 55

Lilianna knocked on the door of the library and pressed a hand to her stomach.

"Come in." The deep male voice almost made her jump.

She took a deep breath, reached for the doorknob and turned.

Barrett stood from behind the desk and narrowed his eyes on her.

"May I have a word with you, sir?"

"Call me Barrett. No one calls me sir." He gestured her inside with a wave of his hand.

She shut the door behind her.

"Have a seat."

"I'd rather stand." She clasp her hands in front of her.

"Still getting used to werewolves, huh?"

"It's not every day I get to see something supernatural."

"Supernatural. I never thought about us being supernatural." He took a drink of his bourbon and sat down behind the desk. "What exactly did you need to talk to me about, Lilianna?"

"Did you force Killian to choose between me and his job?"

He narrowed his eyes. "I did. You'll be happy to know he chose you."

"I know. He told me." Unease snaked through her stomach. "Tell me something, Barrett. What will you do with me? Now that I know about werewolves?" Her eyes widened a little.

"We can't have humans telling the rest of the world about our existence." He leaned his elbows on the desk and steepled his fingers.

"I understand. But what if I had a solution to your problem."

"And what would that be?" He cocked his head.

"You could allow Killian to keep his job as an Assassin and let us be together. That way I have a vested interest in keeping him safe. And you would be ensured that I wouldn't blab to the world."

He snorted. "Until you two had your first disagreement. Then you'd be telling the world what he is…what we all are."

"I wouldn't do that. I would never risk hurting him. I love him." She lifted her chin and held his gaze.

"Being the mate of a Guardian is hard enough. But being a mate to an Assassin is brutal. Would you be okay with him executing the guilty? You saw what he did to those werewolves that were in the basement with you."

"I know that I love him. And I want him to be happy. Being an Assassin makes him happy."

"So do you, according to him." Barrett settle back in the chair. "What would you do while he is on a mission?"

"I'll be waiting for him." She laughed and pressed her hand to her stomach. "And according to Killian, I'll be taking care of a baby."

"He's right. You are pregnant. I can smell it."

She looked at him with surprise. "So it's true."

"Yes. And to be honest, I'm curious about the baby. Werewolves and humans don't mate or have children together. It seems you and Killian are an exception to the rule."

"So it would seem. But I wouldn't just be a housewife. I have plans too. Since Killian lives in New Orleans, I could open my own bakery there. Having my own place has been a dream of mine for a while."

"That's right. You're a baker." He rubbed his chin. "You can bake anything? Cakes, cookies, pies?"

"Yes, anything." She nodded.

He stood behind the desk. "If I give Killian back his job and allow you to mate and marry, would you promise me to bake for Killian so he never has to go anywhere else to get his cookies?"

She frowned. "Sure. Although I don't…"

"Perfect. Now he doesn't have the need for Jacey's cookies. In fact, I know just the place for your bakery. I'll contact the real estate agent." He took a sip of bourbon and slammed the empty glass on the desk. "I'll send Killian in here."

A few minutes passed before the library door opened.

Killian strode inside and scooped her up in his arms. He pressed his lips to hers in a deep kiss.

"What did you say to get Barrett to allow us to mate?"

"Just reasoned with him a little." She smiled and wrapped her arms around his waist. "There was one condition. I have to provide you with all the cookies so you won't have the need to get any cookies from Jacey. Do you know what he meant by that?"

Killian broke out in laugh. "No, sweetheart. I have no idea." He pulled her into his chest and kissed her thoroughly.

"I promise to love you for the rest of my life, Lilliana Beckway."

"And I promise to love you, Killian Black. Forever."

Killian held her tight, making her realize that she'd finally gotten everything in life she had ever dreamed about.

ABOUT THE AUTHOR

Jodi Vaughn is a USA Today best-selling author of over twenty five paranormal romance and contemporary romance novels. She loves writing novels where good always overcomes evil and sometimes the heroine saves the hero.She lives in Northeast Arkansa with her family, three dogs, and two very fickle swans who travel the neighborhood in search of greener pastures.

Sign up for her newsletter at her website jodivaughn.com to keep up with upcoming events, releases, and the latest news!

ALSO BY JODI VAUGHN

The Vampire Housewife Series
Lipstick and Lies and Deadly Goodbyes (book 1)
Merlot and Divorce and Deadly Remorse (book 2)
Bullets and Booze and Dead Suede Shoes (book 3)
Aces and Eights and Dead Werewolf Dates (book 4)

Werewolf Guardian Romance Series
Her Werewolf Bodyguard (book 1)
Her Werewolf Protector (book 2)
Her Werewolf Defender (book 3)
Her Werewolf Champion (book 4)
Her Werewolf Hero (book 5)
Her Werewolf Valentine (book 6)
Her Werewolf Mate (book 7)
Her Werewolf Alpha (book 8)
Her Werewolf Enforcer

Veiled Series
Veiled Secrets (book 1)
Veiled Enchantment (book 2)

Somewhere Texas Series

Saddle Up (book 1)

Trouble in Texas (book 2)

Bad Medicine (book 3)

Somewhere in Paradise (book 4)

Cloverton Series

Christmas in Cloverton

Lost Without You (book 1)

Lost All Control (book 2)

Made in United States
North Haven, CT
03 June 2022

19833884R00133